Friends—Or Rivals?

Amber was next. She sprinted across the mat, leaped like a deer, then sprang forward on her hands. She was almost flying! But halfway through the stunt, she collapsed on the mat.

"You didn't push forward enough," Delight said, performing an effortless handspring.

Amber tried again. And again. Each time she fell over.

"I don't know why I can't get this," she said, scrambling to her feet after her fifth failed handspring. "I can do cartwheels and forward rolls and backward rolls. How come I can't do this?"

The teacher came over to note their progress. "You'll get it," she said. "Just keep practicing. Right, Delight?"

Amber watched Delight do another perfect handspring. Why did Delight have to do everything a little bit better than Amber?

She wondered if she wanted Delight Wakefield for a second-best friend after all.

Third Grade Stars

Candice F. Ransom

SCHOLASTIC INC.

New York   Toronto   London   Auckland   Sydney
Mexico City   New Delhi   Hong Kong   Buenos Aires

ISBN 0-439-65378-9

12 11 10 9 8 7 6 5 4 3 2 1   7 8/0

Printed in the U.S.A.   40

First Scholastic printing, November 2003

Third Grade
Stars

ONE

Amber Cantrell dropped her pencil for the fourth time since her teacher began calling the roll.

She hung over the arm of her desk to pick it up, enjoying the feel of hanging upside down. Her hair swept the floor, she noted with pleasure. Amber had been growing her hair for months. It wasn't quite long enough to sit on yet, but it was getting there.

Maybe it'll be that long by Christmas, she thought hopefully. She wondered how many inches her hair could grow between now, the first day after the Thanksgiving vacation, and Christmas Day. Lost in calculation, she dropped her pencil again.

Mrs. Sharp stopped at David Jackson's name. "Amber," she said, frowning. "Can't you keep hold of that pencil?"

"Sorry." Amber picked up the pencil and laid it firmly on her desk top. She watched it closely so it wouldn't leap off her desk. Today of all days, she wanted to be first in the Monday morning Press Conference. It wouldn't do to make Mrs. Sharp mad.

Across the aisle, Mindy Alexander watched Amber's pencil, too. Mindy was Amber's best friend. She didn't like to see Amber get in trouble.

"Henry Hoffstedder," Mrs. Sharp called, going the wrong way in her roll book.

"You called Henry already," David Jackson said. "You were up to my name. I'm here," he added unnecessarily.

Amber giggled. David Jackson was her on-again, off-again boyfriend. Sometimes Amber liked him. Other times she thought he was a pest. Today she decided she liked him again. David seemed especially cute since they had been out of school for four days.

Mrs. Sharp made a check mark in her book. "I'm so glad you are keeping me on my toes, David. Mondays after a vacation are always difficult." She continued to call the roll until she reached the last name.

"Delight Wakefield."

"Here."

Amber looked over at the girl sitting directly in front of David, on the other side of the room. When she began third grade earlier that year, Amber had been sure of two things. One, she, Amber Gillian Cantrell, would have the prettiest name in her class. And two, she would have the longest hair.

But then Delight Wakefield arrived in Room Six. Delight was a new girl. Her family traveled a lot. Her last school had been in Paris, France.

Right away, Delight took the prize for the prettiest name. She told the class she got her name because her parents had longed for a child. When they finally had a baby girl, they were so delighted that's what they named her.

Even worse, Delight Wakefield had hair long enough to sit on. She was like someone out of a fairy tale. The other kids in the class were fascinated by Delight. David Jackson stared at the new girl more than he made faces at Amber. Even Mindy wanted to be Delight's friend.

Nobody paid any attention to Amber. Whenever Amber tried to be popular, Delight did something better.

When Amber started a stuffed-animal club, so did Delight. Naturally everyone wanted to be in Delight's club. When Amber wanted to be the star of the school pageant, the part went to Delight. Amber couldn't win.

So one day she grabbed a pair of scissors and cut a huge chunk out of Delight's long, beautiful hair.

Remembering this, Amber felt awful. She hadn't meant to ruin Delight's hair. She was just fed up. But then Delight had to get all her hair cut off. Amber had apologized to Delight, but Delight would not be her friend.

Finally Amber gave Delight the thing she loved best in the world, her stuffed raccoon, R.C. She was glad when Delight refused to take R.C. She'd felt even better when she and Delight became friends.

Amber was already best-best friends with Mindy Alexander. But she found there was room in her life for more than one best friend. Delight was Amber's second-best friend. Now Amber and Delight were the most popular kids in Room Six.

Amber noticed that Delight had had her hair cut again during the Thanksgiving vacation. Her honey-colored hair fell in sharp points over her ears. She looked grown-up and important, Amber thought. Delight Wakefield could run for President of the United States with a haircut like that.

Mrs. Sharp closed the roll book. "Press Conference time," she announced. "Who has something worthwhile to contribute?"

Amber raised her hand, nearly tumbling out of her seat with enthusiasm. Me, me, call on me! she silently urged the teacher.

Mrs. Sharp glanced around the room, then nodded at Amber. "Amber, what do you have to share with us this morning?"

Instead of Show-and-Tell, which was for babies, the third-graders held Monday morning Press Conferences. Students could talk about what they did over the weekend, or bring in interesting projects.

Amber walked up to the front of the room. With her back to her classmates, she arranged several tiny objects on Mrs. Sharp's desk. Then she turned around.

"This is R.C.'s Thanksgiving dinner," she explained. "I believe everyone knows my famous stuffed raccoon, R.C. I've brought him to school a few times."

"A few *thousand* times," Henry Hoffstedder said rudely. He was David Jackson's best friend.

"Henry," Mrs. Sharp warned. "Amber, go on."

Henry's remark made Amber lose her place in her speech. She had to start over.

"This is R.C.'s Thanksgiving dinner. Here is his pumpkin pie." She held out a miniature pie made from orange clay. "And this is his turkey drumstick and this is his bread."

She looked up to see if everyone was admiring her clay Thanksgiving food. Only the girls seemed interested. The boys were either yawning or gazing out the window. David Jackson was folding a sheet of notebook paper into a football. He was definitely not paying attention.

Annoyed, Amber concluded her presentation.

"And here is R.C.'s bowl of peas," she said, holding out a tiny clay bowl filled with green clay peas. "The peas were the hardest. They kept rolling away." She turned to the teacher. "That's all."

"Very nice, Amber," Mrs. Sharp said. "We always enjoy seeing your raccoon projects."

"I think it's dumb," said Henry.

"Yeah," David agreed. "Who ever heard of a stuffed raccoon celebrating Thanksgiving?"

Stung, Amber retorted, "How do you know they *don't* celebrate Thanksgiving?"

Mrs. Sharp interrupted. "That's enough, David. Amber, you may sit down. Thank you again."

Gathering the clay objects, Amber sat down in her seat. Her face was red with embarrassment. David knew how much R.C. meant to her. Her father had given the raccoon to her on her sixth birthday, just before he left the family. While her parents were getting divorced, Amber told all her secrets to the stuffed raccoon.

Watching him flick the paper football to Henry Hoffstedder, Amber decided she didn't want David for a boyfriend after all. Their relationship was definitely "off-again."

No one else had any news for the Press Conference, so Mrs. Sharp began lessons.

"We're going to be doing something new in

reading and writing," she said. "Canned book reports."

Amber exchanged a puzzled look with Mindy. Were they going to stuff book reports in tin cans?

"You will read a book every two weeks and do a report," Mrs. Sharp continued.

Henry Hoffstedder groaned.

Amber knew Henry hated to read. She was Henry's reading team partner. The best readers in the class were paired with students who needed extra help in reading. Henry usually spent reading team time fooling around.

"Instead of writing a paragraph describing the book, you will 'can' your reports." Mrs. Sharp went to the supply cupboard and pulled out a big carton filled with empty cans—juice cans, soup cans, green-bean cans.

"What you'll do is take the label off a can and make a new label," the teacher explained. "The title of your book will replace the name of the food. Then you will list the ingredients, which will be the things you liked about the book. Be creative—draw pictures, offer prizes, whatever. We'll talk more about this later, after library period."

"It sounds like fun, doesn't it?" Amber whispered to Mindy.

"You always like to make things," Mindy whispered back. "Look at all those tiny books and catalogs you made for Pearl and R.C."

Last summer Amber had stayed at Mindy's house across the street while her mother worked. Amber and Mindy had been best-best friends since first grade, so Amber didn't mind spending the long summer days at Mindy's.

Amber had brought R.C. and a bag of crayons, markers, paper, and stickers to Mindy's house. When she made R.C. a miniature catalog of the latest raccoon fashions, Mindy wanted one for her stuffed penguin, Pearl.

The girls spent the whole summer making miniature toys, clothes, and books for their stuffed animals. When third grade began in September, they made schoolbooks and worksheets for R.C. and Pearl. Mindy grew tired of creating things, but Amber loved dreaming up new projects, like the Thanksgiving dinner.

Mrs. Sharp answered a few questions about the canned book reports. Next they worked on cursive. They were up to the letter *g* in their workbooks. Amber loved writing capital *G*. So far, it was the most beautiful capital letter in the cursive alphabet. Plus it was a letter she could use. Her middle name was Gillian. She couldn't wait to learn how to write *l*s.

After cursive, it was time for gym.

"Gym," Amber moaned to Mindy. "Yuck!"

"It's not so bad. I like playing soccer."

Mindy was good at sports. She could run fast

and kick a soccer ball hard.

Amber was a slow runner. She couldn't kick a ball farther than two feet. She missed free recess. Last year they could play any game they wanted, or just mess around. But third-graders had gym instead of recess. They played sports, like kickball and soccer.

Delight Wakefield came over so she could stand in line with Amber and Mindy.

"Yucko gym," she said.

"Double-yucko," Amber agreed.

The only good thing about being terrible in gym was that Delight was just as bad. Delight ran even slower than Amber. She couldn't kick a soccer ball very far, either.

"I hope we don't play soccer again," Delight said, smoothing her pointy bangs.

"The last time we played, David Jackson kicked me in the shin," Amber said.

"That's because he likes you."

"Well, he has a funny way of showing it." Secretly, Amber was glad David had kicked her. Still, she'd rather he gave her a flower or something nice.

"I don't like being picked last," Delight said.

"I'll pick you," Mindy offered. She was usually team captain. "Amber first and you second."

"It's too cold to play outside," Mrs. Sharp told the class as they lined up at the door. "We'll be using the indoor gym until the weather is warm again."

Amber cheered up a little. They couldn't play soccer indoors. Maybe the class would have free recess again. She and Mindy and Delight could sit on the bleachers and talk.

When the class was in line, Mrs. Sharp said, "Walk quietly down the hall to the gymnasium. Mrs. Holland will meet you at the door. She has an exciting new unit today."

"What is it?" asked David.

"Mrs. Holland will tell you," Mrs. Sharp said, smiling mysteriously.

"It's probably something awful," Delight said. "With a lot of kicking."

"And running," Amber added. She grinned at Delight. Whatever the new unit was, they were bound to be awful at it.

But Amber didn't mind. She and Delight were the cool girls in Room Six. Even though they were both terrible in sports, the other kids looked up to them. Everyone wanted to sit with Amber and Delight during an assembly, or eat lunch at their table. Lisa and Carly copied everything Amber and Delight did.

Amber walked confidently down the hall. She didn't care that she was no good at sports. Maybe she and Delight would start a new fad. A be-terrible-in-gym fad.

Wouldn't it be funny if *all* the kids in Room Six were terrible in gym?

Chapter TWO

Mrs. Holland met the class at the door. The gym teacher had blonde hair and dimples. Amber liked Mrs. Holland a lot, even if she did teach gym.

"Good morning, people!" Mrs. Holland chirped. "Today we begin gymnastics! By Christmas vacation, you'll all be gymnasts."

David poked Henry. "Sissy stuff," he said in a loud whisper.

"You won't catch me doing that junk," Henry jeered.

Amber had seen a gymnastics competition on TV. There were no balls to kick and very little running involved. But the tricks the gymnasts did looked hard.

First the students changed into gym uniforms,

blue shorts and T-shirts with "Virginia Run Elementary" across the front.

"No shoes," Mrs. Holland told them. "But you can wear socks if you want."

Next she showed them the equipment they would be using. There were thick, blue, foam-filled floor mats.

"Wrestle-mania!" David yelled.

"Not for wrestling," Mrs. Holland said firmly. "The mats will be used for tumbling routines *only*."

She showed them a leather thing that reminded Amber of a horse, only it didn't have a head. Mrs. Holland even called it a pommel horse, although its official name was the vault. Rounding out the equipment was a long, narrow board about four feet off the floor. This was a balance beam.

Mrs. Holland told them they would be doing handstands and flying over the vault and performing tricks on that narrow balance beam.

"I don't think I'm going to like this," Amber said nervously to Mindy.

"Me neither," said Mindy, who normally liked all sports. "I'm too fat to get up on that skinny board."

"No, you're not," Amber said loyally. "We'll probably all be terrible at gymnastics. You, me, Delight. By the way, where is Delight?"

Mindy pointed. "Over there."

Delight had moved away when Mrs. Holland began talking. She seemed very interested in the equipment. As Mrs. Holland described how they would run toward the vault and launch over it, Delight bounced up and down in her pink socks. She looked as if she couldn't wait for her turn.

"We will begin with a simple forward roll," Mrs. Holland said. "This is the easiest routine in gymnastics. *Anyone* can master a forward roll. Now watch me."

The teacher crouched at the edge of a blue mat. She tucked her head into her shoulders, leaned forward on her palms, then tipped over. Like a ball, she rolled over the mat, landing in the same position she started from.

"See?" she said, her face flushed. "Nothing to it. Now, we'll line up by the mats in fives. David, Henry, you boys lead the first group."

She counted off students until five groups were lined up behind the mats.

Amber's group included Mindy, Carly, David, and Henry. Delight was on the other side of the gym with another group.

Amber frowned. What was Delight doing way over there? The others would want to copy them being the worst in the class. She and Delight ought to be in the same group.

"Remember," the teacher instructed. "Tuck in

your chin. Try not to land on your head—"

"Major damage," David quipped. Henry snickered.

"—*or* your neck. You want to place your weight on your shoulders as you roll over." Putting her whistle to her lips, Mrs. Holland blew shrilly. "Let's go!"

David was first. He knelt at the edge of the mat and rolled. Only he didn't roll fast enough and wound up flat on his back with his legs stretched out.

Henry's attempt wasn't much better. He fell over on one shoulder. "Ow," he groaned, struggling to his feet.

Carly was next. Her forward roll wasn't too bad, but she didn't land in the starting position.

Then it was Mindy's turn. She looked at Amber with scared eyes. "I know I can't do this," she whispered. "You go in front of me."

Amber wasn't sure she could do it either. "I'm going to be terrible at this," she said.

She crouched at the edge of the mat. Her knees were under her chin, her head tucked low. Palms flat on the mat, she leaned forward, then rolled. She finished in the starting position. She wasn't terrible after all!

"Yes!" she cried, jumping up and shaking one fist skyward. "Go, Mindy!"

Looking like she had a stomachache, Mindy

squatted on the mat. Her knees did not come as close to her chest as Amber's and her head wasn't low enough. She rolled at an angle, off the mat. David and Henry hooted with laughter.

"Boys!" Mrs. Holland blew her whistle at them. "Are your forward rolls perfect? Keep practicing until you can do a perfect forward roll."

Their group lined up again. Over and over they rolled across the mat. Poor Mindy was terrible. She was just too big to squeeze herself into a ball. The boys horsed around a lot, but they eventually got the hang of it. Carly was pretty good. But no one in their group was as good as Amber.

She could tuck her small body into a tight ball. She *felt* like a ball as she skimmed over the mat. The only thing that bothered her was her hair. It was so long, it tangled as she rolled.

"Now we'll do a *backward* roll," Mrs. Holland said. "You begin in the same position as the forward roll, only you face the other way. Push yourself *backward*. Again, you'll land in the same position as you started. Try not to extend your legs in the middle of the roll."

Amber was anxious for her turn. Mindy eagerly traded places with her. Neither David nor Henry could do a backward roll. Carly kicked her legs halfway through and messed up.

But Amber rolled backward perfectly!

"I don't even want to try," Mindy said.

"Go on," Amber urged. "I'll help you." She crouched beside Mindy on the mat. They pushed backward at the same time. When Amber finished in the starting position, Mindy was lying on her back.

"I can't do it," she moaned.

"Sure you can. It just takes practice."

Mrs. Holland came over to give Mindy extra instruction. Mindy looked even more dejected. The teacher worked with her a few minutes, then went to help another student.

"I hate gym," Mindy said when the teacher couldn't hear.

Amber was surprised. Usually it was Mindy who loved gym. Amber was the one who couldn't run or kick the ball.

Deep down inside, Amber was a tiny bit glad Mindy was having trouble with gymnastics. She didn't want her best friend to be miserable. But it felt great to do forward and backward rolls better than anyone in their group. Maybe even better than anyone in the whole class!

"I hate gym, too," Amber said to keep Mindy company. She didn't really hate gym. In fact, she liked it now. "I bet Delight hates it, too," she added. Maybe Delight was having as much trouble as Mindy.

Delight was performing a backward roll on the last mat. Students from the other groups had gathered around to watch her. Amber and Mindy went over, too.

"Go, Delight!" Amber called encouragingly. Her second-best friend was probably having trouble doing a backward roll. That must be why everyone was watching.

Delight lined up her toes precisely at the edge of the mat. She leaned forward on her palms, then pitched backward. In the middle of her roll, her legs came straight up and her toes pointed toward the ceiling. She held that pose for several seconds, then brought her legs down and finished the roll.

"Too bad," Amber remarked. "You shouldn't have kicked your legs, Delight. If you want, I'll show you how to do it right. Does anybody want to see me do one?"

But the other kids and Mrs. Holland were clapping. Amber couldn't understand why they were applauding a poor backward roll. Were they just trying to make Delight feel better? If so, they should have clapped for Mindy, too.

"Beautiful!" Mrs. Holland praised. "A perfect backward roll with a handstand. That's a more advanced move. It'll be a few weeks before we will try that routine. I'm glad Delight has experience in gymnastics. She'll be a big help to me."

Carly ran up to Delight. "How long have you been doing gymnastics?"

"About two years," Delight replied. "I stopped when we moved here, but now I'm taking lessons again."

Amber's mouth dropped open. Delight Wakefield was taking lessons in gymnastics!

"What else can you do?" asked Lisa. "Can you walk on the balance beam?"

Delight glanced at the teacher. "Is it all right if I do something on the beam?"

"Just this once," Mrs. Holland said. "I don't want anybody fooling around on the equipment without supervision. I will spot you, Delight."

Delight skipped over to the balance beam. Mrs. Holland stood nearby, ready to catch Delight in case she fell. Delight hopped up on the beam with her weight on her hands and her legs straight out in front of her in a V. Slowly she pivoted, then swung her legs up into a handstand. She came down in a forward roll.

Amber was amazed. She couldn't believe the things Delight was doing on that narrow board.

The others were amazed, too. They clapped and whistled when Delight jumped off the beam with her back arched and her arms raised high. Her short hair fell into neat points over her ears. She looked just like the gymnasts in the TV competition.

"Beautiful dismount," Mrs. Holland told her. "Okay, class. Five minutes before the bell. Run to the locker room."

After they had changed, the students clustered admiringly around Delight.

"Ooh, that looks so hard," Carly said.

"Can you do a somersault in the air?" asked Henry.

"Yeah," Delight answered. "But it's tricky!"

Just then the bell rang. It was time for their class to go to lunch.

Lisa pushed Amber out of the way. "Can I sit with you at lunch?" she asked Delight eagerly.

"Me, too!" Carly piped up.

Delight smiled. "Sure. Amber, are you and Mindy coming?"

As the most popular kids in their class, Amber and Delight usually led everyone to the cafeteria. But today Carly and Lisa skipped down the hall with Delight. The boys ran alongside, teasing Delight.

Amber was left behind. Suddenly she didn't feel so popular anymore.

"Hurry up," Mindy said. "There won't be any nachos left."

"I'm coming," Amber said without enthusiasm.

Except for Mindy, no one seemed to care if Amber Cantrell ate lunch or not.

Chapter
THREE

Normally Amber liked Mondays. Monday was Press Conference day and library day, two things Amber loved.

But her presentation at this morning's Press Conference hadn't turned out the way she had hoped. And after that awful gym class, she wasn't in the mood for library period.

"We have to pick out our first book-report book," Mindy said as they filed into the library.

Amber claimed two chairs at the table by the window. She and Mindy sat down. Delight came in and looked around for them. Amber pretended not to see her. Usually Amber, Delight, and Mindy sat together. But Amber was mad at Delight for not saving them seats at lunch.

"There's Delight," Mindy said, waving.

"What happened to you guys at lunch?" Delight asked, sitting down.

"We got to the cafeteria late. Nobody waited for us," Amber replied meaningfully. "We had to sit with the lunch monitor."

"I wanted to wait but Lisa and Carly practically dragged me down the hall," Delight said.

"Did they take our seats?" Amber wanted to know.

"David and Henry did. I tried to save two seats but they just sat down." Delight rolled her eyes. "I wish you *had* been at my table. Henry told awful jokes. I could hardly eat."

Amber laughed. She couldn't stay mad at Delight. It wasn't Delight's fault David and Henry stole the seats meant for Amber and Mindy.

Then Miss Maddox, the librarian, told the third-graders to go look for books.

"I want to read a dog book," Delight said, heading for the animal bookshelf.

"What book are you getting?" Mindy asked Amber.

"I don't know."

"I'm getting a mystery. Why don't you get one, too? Then we can both do mystery cans for our book reports."

"I think I'll just look." Amber headed for the shelves of fact books.

Miss Maddox once had showed her where the books on making things were located. Maybe she would find a book that would give her ideas for R.C.'s Christmas present.

But a book in the sports section caught her eye. The cover showed a girl in a yellow leotard standing on one leg on a balance beam. Her other leg was raised high in the air.

Amber picked up the book. She couldn't read all the words in the title, so she took it to Miss Maddox.

"It's called *The Picture Book of Gymnastics*," Miss Maddox said. "You'll enjoy this one, Amber. Especially since you're doing gymnastics in gym."

Amber took the book over to her table. Mindy and Delight were still searching for books to check out.

Amber opened her book. The first photograph showed the girl in the yellow leotard leaping with her legs in a split. She looked like a beautiful bird.

She turned the page. There was a picture of the girl swinging from wooden bars. The next picture showed her bending backward. Her back made an upside-down U.

The pictures were all of the same girl doing impossible feats. In the background, an audience watched her perform. Everyone's eyes were fixed on the girl in the yellow leotard. She was obviously the star.

Amber closed the book, hugging it to her chest. More than anything, she decided, she longed to be like that flying, graceful girl in the yellow leotard. Suddenly, being a gymnast was more important than having the longest hair or the prettiest name in third grade. She wanted to be a star, too!

Five minutes before library period was over, the class lined up to have their books checked out. Amber stood in line behind David and Henry, who were talking loudly about their books.

"I got *Reptiles of the World*," David said. "I want to be a snake scientist when I grow up."

"Sounds like you," Amber said. She was still mad at him for making cracks about R.C. earlier. *And* for stealing her seat at lunch.

David punched her arm. "At least I won't still be playing with baby stuffed animals. When you're grown up, you'll be driving with that stupid raccoon on the seat beside you. You'll probably take him to college!"

"She'll probably marry him!" Henry put in. Both boys sputtered with laughter.

"At least I won't be crawling around on the ground," Amber returned.

"Hey, that's the only way to find snakes. And when I find one, I'm going to throw him on you!" David tossed an invisible snake at Amber.

She shrieked. Miss Maddox looked over and gave her a stern glance.

"We need to think of a name for our club," David said to Henry.

"What kind of club is it?" Amber asked him. She wondered if he would let her be in it.

"It's not a stuffed-animal club," Henry said.

"I wasn't asking *you,*" Amber said coldly.

David answered her question. "It's a snake club. We're going to catch snakes and lizards and reptiles. You're good at naming things. Can you think of a cool name for our snake club?"

Amber shivered. Why did boys like such icky things? Still, she *was* good at naming things.

"How about the Lizard Men?" she suggested.

"Lizard Men," David echoed. "Not bad. What do you think, Hoffstedder?"

"Nah. Let's call ourselves the Cobras," Henry said.

David looked apologetically at Amber. "I like Henry's name better. But yours was good, too."

Amber shrugged. She didn't want to be in David's dumb old club anyway.

Just then Delight and Mindy came over.

Delight showed Amber her book about an Irish setter. "I love Irish setters," she said. "I wish my mom would let me have one." Then she noticed Amber's book. "Oh, that's a good one. I read it a long time ago."

"Can you do this?" Amber pointed to the girl in the yellow leotard on the cover.

Delight nodded. "Yes. But I took a lot of

lessons before I could."

"I couldn't do that if I took a million lessons," Mindy said.

"Sure you could," Delight said. "All it takes is practice."

"And a skinny body, like you and Amber have." Mindy pretended she was standing on a balance beam. She leaned to one side and toppled over.

Delight laughed, but Amber was busy thinking.

Delight was good at gymnastics because she took lessons. If Amber took lessons, she'd be good too! As soon as she got home from school, she was going to ask her mother for gymnastics lessons.

When Amber walked into her house that afternoon, her brother came out of the kitchen. He had on headphones and was eating an apple. A dish-towel was slung over one shoulder.

"You have to clean your room, fold the laundry, and take out the garbage," Justin informed her. He wiggled his hips in time to a beat only he could hear.

"Who says?" Amber dropped her knapsack on the floor with a thump. Then, realizing her brother couldn't hear her, she yelled, "WHO SAYS?"

He pulled off his headphones. "Mom says. She called. She'll be late tonight."

Justin was thirteen. He was always bossing Amber around.

"I told Mindy I'd go over to her house," Amber said.

On the bus ride home, she and Mindy and Delight had planned to read their books together.

"You can go over to Mindy's *after* you have done your chores," Justin replied heartlessly. "If you have time."

"I don't believe Mom told you I have to do all those things," Amber protested. "I'm going to call her." She headed for the phone in the kitchen.

"I wouldn't do that if I were you," Justin said behind her. "Mom's working late and she didn't sound happy about it."

Mrs. Cantrell owned a shop that sold old and new handmade quilts. The shop was called A Stitch in Time. Usually Amber's mom worked a half day on Mondays and was home by the time Amber got back from school.

Justin was probably right. Their mother wouldn't be in a very good mood if she had to work late. It wouldn't do any good for Amber to call her and complain.

"What are *you* supposed to do?" she demanded. "Listen to music and eat while I slave?"

Her brother flipped his apple core over her head. "I have to fix supper. I'm going to make the Cantrell Specialty—Pickle Pizza," he said grandly.

Pizza was the only thing Justin could cook.

Usually he put peppers and onions on a plain frozen pizza. But once when he didn't have any peppers, he dumped a jar of dill pickles on top. Justin loved his creation, but it made Amber sick.

She clutched her stomach at the mention of Pickle Pizza. "Yuck! I just want a peanut butter sandwich."

"Mom also said you have to eat whatever I make." With a flick of the dishtowel, Justin swaggered into the kitchen.

Amber called Mindy and told her she wouldn't be over until later. Maybe not at all. Then she tackled the chores.

First she took the garbage bag out to the garage and stuffed it in a black plastic sack. Justin would carry it out to the curb after supper.

Next she dumped the laundry basket on the sofa and began folding clothes. After putting folded laundry on each person's bed, she went into her room.

Her room was very messy. She had left for school that morning in a big hurry. The tulip quilt her mother had made her lay in a tangled heap at the foot of her bed. Sneakers tumbled out of the closet. Her desk was a jumble of books, crayons, construction paper, and craft supplies. Globs of clay from R.C.'s Thanksgiving project were stuck to the floor.

Her stuffed raccoon smiled at her from his place on her pillow.

"Why can't you be a magic raccoon?" she accused. "Why can't you straighten my room while I'm at school?"

Then she went over and gave her raccoon a big hug. She didn't want to hurt R.C.'s feelings, just in case he *had* feelings. Besides, R.C. was her truest friend in the world. He didn't care if she wasn't the most popular girl in third grade. He liked her just the way she was.

With a sigh, Amber began picking up shoes. She worked in her room until she heard the front door close with the determined thump that meant her mother was home at last.

Amber ran out to the living room.

"Hi, Mom!" she greeted. "How was your day?"

She wanted to bring up gymnastics lessons, but knew better than to ask her mother for any favors the instant she came home from work. She had learned to wait until her mother had a chance to "wind down."

Normally Mrs. Cantrell took off her shoes and rested a few minutes in the recliner. But tonight she kissed Amber hello in a distracted manner, then went into the kitchen.

"What's for dinner?" Mrs. Cantrell asked Justin.

He opened the oven door, grinning proudly. "My specialty—Pickle Pizza!"

"Sounds great." Mrs. Cantrell emptied her tote bag onto the kitchen table. There were a lot of envelopes with windows. Amber knew they were bills. She also knew something was wrong. Her mother didn't like Pickle Pizza either.

"I think we have some leftover pasta salad," Mrs. Cantrell said, fishing in the refrigerator. "And a few of those sourdough rolls from last night's dinner. They'll taste good with your pizza, Justin."

Amber helped herself to pasta salad. Her mother knew she couldn't eat Justin's gross pizza. This way, his feelings wouldn't be hurt.

"How was school?" Mrs. Cantrell asked them.

Justin rambled on about a field trip his class was taking. Amber noticed her mother was only half-listening.

"And how was your day?" her mother asked Amber when Justin had finished.

"Okay," Amber said simply. Somehow she didn't think her mother was really interested. She sensed it wasn't the right time to ask about gymnastics lessons.

She found out what was bothering her mother after they had eaten.

"I have an announcement," Mrs. Cantrell said. "I'm going to be working longer hours."

"Why?" Justin asked.

"Elizabeth left today," Mrs. Cantrell answered. "She's not my business partner anymore."

Elizabeth owned the quilt shop with Mrs.

Cantrell and worked in the shop evenings and a half day on Mondays.

"So you don't have a business partner anymore?" Justin said.

"No." Mrs. Cantrell sighed. "I'm sorry, kids. I don't like being away from you so much."

"Will you have to work late every night?" Amber asked, concerned. If her mother was always at the shop, who would drive Amber to gymnastics lessons?

"I might hire someone to help out in the store," her mother replied. "But I can't afford to do that yet." She sifted through the pile of envelopes. "We'll have to tighten our belts around here for a while, guys."

"Does this mean we're poor?" Amber worried that they would have to eat Pickle Pizza every night.

Her mother smiled. "We'll be fine, but we can't splurge on luxuries."

Justin snapped his fingers. "Darn! I guess I'll have to cancel that Porsche 911 I ordered."

Mrs. Cantrell laughed. "I knew I could count on you!"

Amber pushed the remains of her pasta salad around her plate. She didn't dare ask her mother for gymnastics lessons now. Still, there was her *father*....

While her mother rinsed the dishes, Amber slipped into the living room and dialed her father's number.

Mr. Cantrell lived in an apartment in Maryland.

Amber knew her mother and father were divorced, but she didn't understand why her father had to live so far away. He could have stayed in Virginia. Amber and Justin were supposed to visit their father every other weekend.

Lately Mr. Cantrell had canceled several weekend visits. This was because he had a lady friend in Philadelphia. He went to see her most weekends now.

But over the Thanksgiving holiday, Amber and Justin had been with their father for two whole days. He took them out to eat at a seafood restaurant. When Amber had hesitated over the menu, her father had said, "My little girl can have anything she wants."

Amber knew her father would want her to have gymnastics lessons. All she had to do was ask him.

He answered on the twelfth ring. He sounded like he was a million miles away.

Suddenly shy, Amber twisted the phone cord. "Daddy? This is Amber."

"Oh, hi, pumpkin. What's up?"

"Umm . . ." She couldn't blurt out her request. She would have to lead into it. "Are you coming over this weekend?"

Her father's voice became apologetic. "I'm sorry, Amber, but I'm going to Philadelphia. Ruth and I have tickets for a play." Ruth was her father's lady friend.

"Will I see you the *next* weekend?"

"I'm afraid it'll be a few weeks before I can take you and Justin for the whole weekend."

"How come?" Her heart sank. She missed her father.

"Well, Ruth wants me to do some work around her house. I need to do it before it snows. It's very cold in Pennsylvania, you know." He added brightly, "But I'll come by after work this week. I promise. We'll go out for ice cream."

"When?" Amber asked.

"Thursday. Is that okay?"

"Okay." Amber was glad she'd see her father in a few days. Now she didn't want to ask him for gymnastics lessons over the phone. It would be better to wait until she saw him.

"I have to go now," she told him.

Her father made kissing sounds into the phone. "Tell Justin I said hi. See you both Thursday."

Amber slowly hung up the phone. Her father was busy with his new girlfriend. Maybe he wouldn't be interested in dumb old gymnastics lessons. And she couldn't bother her mother, since they were all tightening their belts.

How would she ever get gymnastics lessons?

FOUR

That night Amber went to bed early. Snuggling up with R.C., she read her library book. A lot of the words in the book were too big to understand, but she studied the pictures.

The girl who became a gymnast worked very hard. She took lessons for years, beginning when she was a little girl. And she practiced every day.

Amber wouldn't mind working hard. If that's what it took to be a star, she'd gladly practice *twice* a day. It would be worth it to perform in front of hundreds of people, all clapping for her.

She dozed with her light on and the book tented across her chest. When her mother came in to kiss her good night, she was barely awake. Mrs. Cantrell put the book on Amber's nightstand and switched off the lamp.

"Mom," Amber murmured.

Her mother turned from the door. "I thought you were asleep."

"I called Daddy this evening," she confessed. "It's a long-distance call. I forgot we're supposed to tighten our belts."

Her mother came over and touched her cheek. "It's okay, honey. You can still talk to your father."

"Daddy can't come this weekend. Or the weekend after that," Amber said. "He's going to see that lady in Philadelphia. I wish he'd remember he's supposed to see us."

"He doesn't mean to forget," her mother said. "It's just that your father has other people in his life right now."

"Who else besides that lady?"

Her mother pulled the quilt up around her neck. "New friends. It's as if you moved to a new neighborhood and went to a new school. You'd try to see your old friends, but you'd have new ones to spend time with, too."

"I'm not Daddy's friend."

"No, you're his daughter. You're very special, and he loves you very much. So do I. Remember that." She kissed Amber good night.

Amber turned over, putting R.C. on the pillow beside her, and fell asleep. She dreamed she was flying through the air in a bright yellow leotard. Down below, her father was clapping for her.

The next day in gym class they learned to do cartwheels.

Mrs. Holland asked Delight to demonstrate. Amber realized that Delight would always be asked to demonstrate because she took lessons.

"Keep your weight on your right leg, then bend to the side, shifting your weight to your left leg," the teacher instructed. "Put your left hand on the mat and kick that right leg! Then put the other hand on the mat and kick your left leg! Don't stop in midair or you'll fall over."

Delight performed a perfect cartwheel, her toes pointed like the professional gymnast in Amber's book. She could even do a cartwheel with only one hand.

"Beautiful, Delight," Mrs. Holland praised. "This movement is four counts. Hand-hand-foot-foot. Now let's try it. Line up in fives."

Amber already knew how to do a cartwheel, so she decided to show off a little. Instead of doing just one, she did three in a row across the mat. She finished with her hands on her hips.

Mindy was impressed. "That was great, Amber. You make it look easy."

"It is easy. Go on."

But Mindy didn't kick her legs high enough.

She fell sideways, sprawled across the mat. A number of kids were having this problem. Mrs. Holland called those students together to give them extra help.

Amber went over to Delight. "Where do you take gymnastics?" she asked.

"At Tumbling Kids. It's next to our grocery store," Delight replied.

Amber's mother went to the same grocery store. Amber had never noticed a gymnastics school there before. "When do you go?"

"Every Tuesday after school, and Saturdays in the afternoon. They have beginner classes in the morning."

"How come you didn't tell Mindy and me you were taking gymnastics lessons?" Amber said. "I thought we were friends."

"We are! It's just—" Delight stared at her feet. "If you want to know the truth, I don't want to take lessons anymore. I'd rather come to your house on Saturdays. I miss doing stuff with you and Mindy. That's a lot more fun than gymnastics."

"Why don't you quit?" Amber said. If Delight gave up *her* lessons, and Amber began taking gymnastics, then *Amber* would be the best gymnast in third grade.

"I can't. My mom says I should go another year. Next year I can take ballet if I want." She did a clumsy spin with her arms over her head.

Amber laughed. She really liked Delight. But Amber was determined to be as good as Delight in gymnastics. She had to think of a way to take lessons!

After school, Amber did her chores without complaint. She put clothes in the dryer, swept the kitchen, and helped Justin with supper, thinking all the while.

Delight had mentioned a beginner class on Saturday mornings. That was probably the class Amber ought to take.

The hardest part, she decided, would be getting a ride to Tumbling Kids every week. Saturday was her mother's busiest day at the quilt shop. She wouldn't be able to drive Amber to Tumbling Kids. The shopping center was only a few miles away, but it was too far to walk or ride her bike.

Then Amber remembered the city buses that cruised up and down the highway like green-and-gold dinosaurs. She and Justin often took those buses to the library. The same bus went to the shopping center.

Amber had never ridden the city bus by herself, but she was sure she could. She had some money left from her allowance. She could use that for bus fare.

While her brother was busy stirring a disgusting mess of peas and corned beef hash, Amber happily set the table. Justin was playing his music so loud, he never noticed that Amber was humming her own tune. She couldn't wait until Saturday.

On Saturday morning, her mother left early to open the shop. Amber and her brother went with Mrs. Cantrell to the door.

"Don't stay too long at Mindy's," Mrs. Cantrell said to Amber. She believed Amber was playing at Mindy's house.

"I won't," Amber replied truthfully. She wasn't going to Mindy's at all. The Alexanders were going to Culpeper to visit Mindy's grandmother.

Her mother started the engine of their station wagon. "Justin, take care of things. I'll see you around six-thirty. We'll go out for hamburgers, okay? Amber, mind your brother."

"Yeah, Amber," Justin said, as they watched the car back out of the driveway. "You have to listen to me." He danced back to his room.

Amber went to her own room for her jacket and purse. "I'm leaving now," she called to Justin through his closed door. "I'll be back after lunch." She didn't know how long the gymnastics class would last, but she should be back by then.

"Uh-huh," her brother mumbled, clearly not interested.

Amber closed the front door behind her and walked down Carriage Street to the corner of Stone Road. A green-and-gold sign marked the bus stop.

She waited in front of the sign, holding tightly to her red plastic purse. The purse had a Scottie dog pocket on the front. In the Scottie pocket were three quarters and two dimes. Amber hoped that would be enough money to ride the bus to the shopping center and back.

No one else waited at the stop with her. She counted blackbirds sitting on the telephone wire. Then she counted the cracks in the sidewalk as far as she could see. After thirty-five blackbirds and fifteen cracks, the bus finally came.

The door opened with a whoosh and Amber stepped up.

"How much?" she whispered to the driver.

"That depends on where you are going," he answered.

"To the shopping center with our grocery store," she replied.

"You mean the Giant on Lee Highway?"

Amber nodded.

"That's just the next stop. Twenty-five cents, please"

She dropped a quarter into the slot of the glass box. Then she found a seat and looked around. There were only two other passengers, an old woman wearing a white knitted cap and a teenage boy who had his feet on the seat across from his.

It was a short ride to the shopping center. The

bus driver told Amber, "Your stop, Miss."

She climbed off the bus and waved at him. He was very nice. So far this trip was a breeze!

The shopping center was Saturday-morning busy. Cars pulled into and out of parking spaces. Wire baskets clanked in front of the grocery store.

Amber walked past the grocery store until she came to a door with a picture of a gymnast painted on the glass. This must be Tumbling Kids.

She pushed open the door. Inside was a small room with a desk. Several little girls in blue leotards ran around. Just beyond the small room was a large room. Long mirrors hung on the walls. Blue mats covered the wooden floor. More little girls tumbled on the mats.

Amber looked at them with dismay. They were *very* young, younger than Mindy's little sister Karen, who was four. Was this the beginner class? She didn't want to be in a class with babies.

A woman with a clipboard and glasses on a neck chain came over to Amber. "May I help you, young lady?"

"I want—is that the beginner class?" Amber asked, pointing to the little kids.

"That is our preschool tumbling class," the woman replied. "Beginning gymnastics is in here." She led Amber to another door.

This room looked like the other room, only

there were a balance beam and pommel horse to one side. Girls Amber's age were flipping and performing on the mats.

Amber let out a sigh of relief. This was her class!

"Are you a new student?" the woman asked her.

"Yes." She smiled. "Can I sign up today?"

"Certainly." The woman went to the desk and pulled out a form. "Your parents will have to fill this out. Are they with you today?"

"My mother is at work. My father is in Philadelphia."

Now the woman put on her glasses and looked at Amber. "Your mother is not with you?"

"She's at her shop. It's her busiest day. Can't I take the form home to her like I do in school? I'll bring it back tomorrow."

The woman shook her head. "I'm afraid that's against our policy. Your mother must fill out this form and pay your tuition in person. In fact, I need to talk to her, to find out your level of experience in gymnastics."

"I want to take a class today," Amber cried. "I came on the bus and everything!"

"I'm sorry," the woman said. "But without your mother's permission and tuition—that's payment—you can't possibly take a class. The studio has rules, you know."

"But—"

The woman walked her to the door. "Come back with your mother. We'll be happy to sign you up then."

Amber found herself outside Tumbling Kids. With leaden steps, she trudged back to the bus stop. It seemed like she couldn't do anything without her mother's permission.

She waited for the bus. And waited. And *waited*. Her feet were numb with cold.

Finally a boy on a bicycle pedaled past. "Hey, kid," he said. "That bus doesn't run anymore today."

"What? You mean it won't come?"

"That's right. Today's Saturday. Can't you read the sign?"

In very small letters under the green-and-gold symbol were some numbers. Amber hadn't even noticed them before. Obviously the bus wasn't coming.

Tears stung her eyes. *Now* what was she going to do? She didn't have enough money for a taxi. But she did have enough left for a telephone call. Maybe she could call Mindy's mother to come get her. Then she remembered Mindy and her family were in Culpeper visiting Mindy's grandmother.

She could call Justin. But what could he do, besides yell at her? He couldn't drive. And it was too far to walk home.

There was only one person to call. Amber located the phone booth. Standing on tiptoe, she dropped her quarter into the phone and dialed the number of her mother's shop.

When her mother answered, Amber began to cry.

"Mom!" she wailed. "I'm at the shopping center and I missed the bus! I can't get home!"

"*What* shopping center?" her mother asked.

"The one with our grocery store."

"I'll be right there, Amber. Wait inside the Giant. It's warmer there."

She hung up and went inside the grocery store. A few minutes later, her mother's station wagon pulled up in front. Amber ran out and gratefully climbed into the car.

"Are you all right?" her mother said.

Amber nodded. She knew her mother was angry. She'd had to leave her shop on her busiest day. And Amber was not at Mindy's, as she had led her mother to believe.

"Okay," her mother said as they drove down Lee Highway. "Out with it. What were you doing on the bus?"

Amber told her mother the whole story: that she had lied about going to Mindy's, and that she had taken a bus to the shopping center to sign up for gymnastics lessons, only they wouldn't let her.

Her mother sighed. "Oh, Amber. I could have told you the city bus has a different schedule on weekends. And of course you need me to sign up for any kind of class."

"I didn't know that." Amber sniffled. "I wanted to take gymnastics lessons but I didn't want to bother you."

At home, her mother went straight to Justin's room. "Justin, is this how you watch your little sister?" she accused.

He stared at Amber. "What do you mean? Wasn't she at Mindy's?"

"No. She took the bus to the shopping center. Without my knowledge or permission. I had to close the shop and go get her."

"What a dumb thing to do," Justin said to Amber.

Mrs. Cantrell put her hands on her hips. "I am disappointed in both of you. Justin, your job is to watch Amber. And Amber, you should act more responsibly. Everyone in this family must be a team player or we will lose the game!"

Ashamed, Amber retreated into her room. Digging out her crayons and paper, she made her mother a card. On the front was a picture of R.C., with his tail drooping sadly. On the inside she wrote, *I'm sorry*.

She took the card to her mother, who was

sitting at the kitchen table with a cup of coffee.

"I made this for you," she said, giving the card to her.

Her mother opened the card and smiled. "I'm sorry, too," she said, kissing Amber. "I'm sorry I blew my top. I want to be home with you and Justin, but I need to be at the shop. I can't be in two places at once."

"I'm sorry I made you close the shop to come get me," Amber said. "I know Saturday is your busiest day."

"Not lately, it isn't," her mother said with a sad smile. "Business has been very slow, even on Saturday. I guess people can't afford to buy handmade quilts these days."

Her mother propped the card on the table so they all could enjoy it. Amber looked at the card. She felt as sad as the raccoon in the picture.

R.C. was sitting on the breakfast bar stool, where Amber had left him that morning. She picked him up and hugged his soft, squishy body.

R.C. didn't hug her back. He couldn't. He was only a stuffed animal.

Amber met Mindy as she was coming out of her house across the street.

"Ready to 'can' our book reports?" Amber asked.

Mindy held up a sack. "I've got the cans. Delight's supposed to have everything else."

Delight had invited them over to work on their canned book reports together. It was a short walk down Carriage Street, over Little Rocky Run, to Delight's house in Mockingbird Ridge.

Mindy was right, Amber thought. Delight *did* have everything. She had both parents living in the same house, and gymnastics lessons she didn't even want. Delight probably even had a yellow leotard.

Delight's house was a lot bigger and newer than Amber's and Mindy's. The Wakefields had already decorated for Christmas. There were tiny white lights twinkling in the bushes on either side of the driveway. A huge pine-cone wreath nearly covered the front door.

Mrs. Wakefield let them in. "Hi, girls," she said, taking their coats and scarves. "Delight's in the family room. Go on down."

The Wakefields' family room looked like an appliance store. Lining the walls were a huge television set, VCR, stereo, and a computer. There was even a tiny kitchen in one corner.

Delight was waiting for them at the big round table. She had assembled supplies for their projects: markers, pens, construction paper, glue, glitter, crayons, pipe cleaners, and fabric scraps.

"Hi, guys. Anybody want a soda?" She went to the tiny refrigerator and pulled out a bottle of soda. Amber marveled at the miniature ice tray and decided that R.C. ought to have a little refrigerator that made tiny ice cubes.

"No thanks. I'm not thirsty now," Amber said. She put her library book on the table with Mindy's.

"We just ate," Mindy added.

Delight put away the bottle. "I don't get this project. Do you understand what the teacher wants us to do, Amber?"

"Sure. We read a book and then instead of telling what the book was about, we say it on a food label. What's so hard about that?" Amber made it sound as if the canned book report was the easiest thing in the world.

Mindy and Delight just looked at her. "I don't get it either," Mindy said. "What's that business with the ingredients?"

Amber began passing out construction paper to each of them. "All you do is write down the things you liked about the book and put a number after each one. Like if the book was really exciting, you say 'Exciting—80 percent.'"

"I can't even *spell* 'exciting,'" Mindy said.

"Spelling counts," Delight said. "Mrs. Sharp said so. She gave us that sheet with words on it." She dug around in the pile of papers and came up with a copy.

"Write what you want to say on a piece of paper first, and then make your label," Amber advised. "That way you won't mess it up."

The girls began scribbling ideas on scrap paper. Then they cut out labels to fit the cans they had chosen. Amber selected a coffee can so she would have plenty of room for illustrations.

She drew a girl wearing a yellow leotard for the front of her label. The girl had long brown hair streaming out behind her as she did a flip in the air. Carefully Amber lettered the title of her book around the label. She showed the drawing to Delight.

"It's good," Delight pronounced. "But the hair is wrong. You don't have long hair in gymnastics. It gets in the way."

"What did you do when you had long hair?" Amber asked. She never mentioned the fact that she had cut off Delight's hair a few months ago. That was why Delight had such short hair now.

"My mom pinned it up," Delight replied. "Is that supposed to be you?"

"No," Amber said quickly. "It's just a girl." But it *was* her. More than anything, Amber wanted to wear a yellow leotard and fly through the air doing stunts. She would even pin up her hair. Then she asked Delight, "Do you have a yellow leotard?"

Delight shook her head. "No. I have a red one and a blue one. Why?"

"I thought maybe I didn't draw it right." Secretly Amber was glad Delight didn't have a yellow leotard.

They were silent a while, working on their book report labels.

Amber glued red glitter to the background of her label. She wrote the ingredients on the back: "Excitement: 50%, Action: 60%, Makes You Want to Turn the Pages: 10%."

She frowned. The numbers had to add up to one hundred. Hers added up to 120. She changed the 60 percent to 45 percent, and the 10 percent to 5 percent. Now the numbers added up to one hundred. Her label was finished. But it wasn't very exciting.

Suddenly she had an idea. She traced the figure of the gymnast on her label onto another piece of paper and colored it. After cutting out the second figure, she glued a pipe cleaner to the back where it wouldn't show. Then she glued the other end of the pipe cleaner to the figure she had drawn on her label.

When the glue was dry, the figure on the label stuck out from the can. It seemed to jump and turn, like a real gymnast.

Ordinarily Amber showed off her creations immediately. This time she tried to hide her project so the others wouldn't see. But it was too late.

Delight noticed Amber's jiggling gymnast. "Ooh, isn't that cute! Will you fix mine like that?"

"Mine, too," Mindy chimed. "I want a dancing figure on my label, too."

"Your reports aren't like mine," Amber said. "My book is about gymnastics. Mindy, yours is a ghost story."

"I put a ghost on the front of my label. Make my ghost dance and wiggle. Please, Amber?"

Delight shoved her own label across the table. "I didn't draw anything on my label because I can't draw very well. But I made fancy letters. I read *Big Red*. You can make the big capital *B* move. Won't that look neat?"

Amber took her friends' labels reluctantly. She didn't want to make Mindy's and Delight's labels dance and move like hers. Then all their labels would look the same. She wanted hers to be unique. An Amber Gillian Cantrell original.

"I wish I could think up the neat things Amber does," Mindy was saying to Delight. "She always has the best ideas."

"We'll have the only labels with moving parts," Delight said happily. "The other kids will be so jealous."

With a sigh, Amber began tracing the ghost on Mindy's label. Even though she wanted to have the only project with a dancing figure, she couldn't disappoint her friends.

On the bottom of Mindy's ghost, and in one corner of Delight's capital *B*, Amber added something extra. She printed her name in very tiny letters. This way anyone who looked closely would know the dancing figure was Amber's creation.

The next day, Mrs. Sharp collected the book reports. The students went to the front of the room and dropped their cans into a wicker laundry basket.

"I see I'll have some interesting reading when I get home tonight. They all look very appetizing!" Mrs. Sharp joked as Delight's row came up to hand in their cans.

Delight's project lay on top of the pile in the basket. Mrs. Sharp reached in and picked it up.

"Isn't this clever?" She made the *B* on Delight's label wiggle, then peered at the bottom to check the student's name. "This is Delight's project. See, class? It has a 3-D effect."

Everyone exclaimed over the dancing *B*.

Amber turned to Mindy. "It was *my* idea! Why doesn't Mrs. Sharp look at *my* can?"

She glanced over at Delight. What kind of a friend was she? A *real* friend wouldn't hog all the credit.

Just then Delight spoke up. "Mrs. Sharp, Amber did that to her label and she helped Mindy and me do ours the same way. Amber's is really the cutest. You should see hers."

Amber straightened in her seat. Now everyone would see that Amber's can was the best.

But Mrs. Sharp put the basket in the corner. "We don't have time to go through all the cans now," she said. "Let's open our math workbooks to page fifty-seven."

Glumly, Amber opened her workbook. No one would ever know that her can was the cutest.

After math, it was time to line up for gym. As they walked down the hall, Carly and Lisa clustered around Delight. They practically pushed Amber out of the way.

"Your can was so cute," Carly said. "You'll get an A for sure."

Amber felt angry. Why did Delight have to get all the attention? It wasn't fair!

"Amber will get an A-plus," Delight said. "Hers is really the best, because she can draw so well."

Lisa nodded. "Amber is a good artist. I loved those little books and magazines you made for your raccoon, Amber. I tried making some for my Barbie doll, but they weren't as cute as the ones you did."

"I just like making things," Amber said modestly. "I've been doing it for years."

The five girls walked into the gym together. They formed the first group at the blue mats.

"Today we're going to try front handsprings," Mrs. Holland announced. "This is a pretty advanced move, but I think you guys can handle it. Delight, will you demonstrate for me?"

Delight got into position. She ran forward, gave a little jump, then sprang onto her hands, flipping over neatly. She moved so fast, she looked like she was flying.

Amber couldn't wait to try it.

The students lined up at the mats.

"Remember to keep your legs together when you are in the air," Mrs. Holland instructed. "You'll need the momentum to land on your feet. Okay, people, let's go."

Carly and Mindy were too nervous, so Lisa went first. She managed to get her legs halfway into the air, then tumbled down.

"It's *hard!*" Lisa said, going to the end of the line.

Amber was next. She sprinted across the mat, leaped like a deer, then sprang forward on her hands. She was almost flying! But halfway through the stunt, she collapsed on the mat.

"You didn't push forward enough," Delight said, performing an effortless handspring.

Amber tried again. And *again.* Each time she fell over.

"I don't know why I can't get this," she said, scrambling to her feet after her fifth failed handspring. "I can do cartwheels and forward rolls and backward rolls. How come I can't do this?"

The teacher came over to note their progress. "You'll get it," she said. "Just keep practicing. Right, Delight?"

Amber watched Delight do another perfect handspring. Why did Delight have to do everything a little bit better than Amber?

She wondered if she wanted Delight Wakefield for a second-best friend after all.

Mrs. Cantrell's car was in the driveway when Amber got home from school.

She burst into the house. Her mother was in the kitchen stirring spaghetti sauce. At least they wouldn't have Pickle Pizza tonight!

"How come you're early?" Amber asked her mother.

"I had an appointment at the bank," her mother replied. "I'm going back to the shop after supper, to put up Christmas decorations. Want to come help?"

"Sure." Decorating the shop was fun.

She climbed on the stool next to the counter. "When are we going to decorate our house? Delight's mother fixed their house up already."

"I know. I've driven by the Wakefields'. Delight's mother always makes their place look so nice." Her mother sighed. "I guess we can get the tree this weekend. That's probably all we'll do this year."

"We aren't putting that green stuff on the bannister?" Amber asked. "Or fixing up the birds' tree in the backyard?" Those were things they had always done.

"I'm sorry, sweetie, but I just don't have the time." Mrs. Cantrell smiled. "Why don't you and Justin fix up the house? Surprise me!"

Decorating the house with her brother wouldn't be much fun. Justin would boss her around and make her do all the dirty work.

The phone rang. Mrs. Cantrell answered it.

Justin came in to snitch a cookie. He gave Amber a signal to follow him into the living room.

"Give Mom a break," he said to her. "She's having a really tough time now."

"What happened?"

"She went to the bank to get a loan and they turned her down."

"They wouldn't give her any money?" Amber didn't understand much about finances.

"No. Mom might lose the shop," Justin said grimly.

Amber knew that would be terrible. Her mother loved her quilt shop. She loved making beautiful quilts and going around the countryside to buy old, handmade quilts to sell in her shop along with the new ones.

Just then Mrs. Cantrell came in. "That was your father. He's coming by for a few minutes after supper." She went back into the kitchen.

Amber's hopes suddenly rose. Tonight she would ask her father about gymnastics lessons. The last time she talked to him she had chickened out. And after the time she took the bus alone to Tumbling Kids, she'd been afraid to bring up the subject again to her mother.

"Since Dad's coming over," Amber said to Justin, "I'm going to dress R.C. in the new outfit I made him."

"He's not coming to see your raccoon," Justin said. "He's coming to bring Mom her support check. He knows she needs the money. I think he wants to help her with the shop."

"How do you know all this?"

"I pay attention, that's how." He punched her lightly. "Try it sometime."

Amber and her mother were clearing the supper table when the doorbell rang. Amber thought it was funny that her father rang the doorbell, like a stranger. He used to *live* in their house.

She ran to answer the door.

Her father scooped her up in a smothering hug. "Hello, pumpkin. Got a kiss for your old dad?"

She kissed him loudly on the cheek. "Got anything for me?" Usually her father brought her and Justin little presents when he came to pick them up for their weekend visits.

"I don't know," he said, digging in the pockets of his down vest. "Let me check."

Amber hopped up and down. Wouldn't it be funny if he had a yellow leotard in his pocket?

Mr. Cantrell pulled out a handkerchief. "How about this?"

"Ewwww!" Amber wrinkled her nose. "I'll check myself." She thrust her hand into the deep pocket. Her fingers closed over something stiff and thin, like a card. She pulled it out.

It was a photograph, a school picture, of a girl about Amber's age. The girl had red hair in two ponytails and a wide grin. She looked like she was about to burst into giggles.

Amber turned the picture over. "Love, Jessie" was printed neatly on the back.

She looked up at her father. "Who's this kid?"

"That's Jessie. Jessica," he replied. "Ruth's daughter." Ruth was her father's lady friend in Philadelphia. "She's in the third grade, too."

"Do you see Jessie when you go to Philadelphia?" Amber wanted to know.

"Yeah. She lives with her mother."

Her father went to see this kid named Jessica every weekend now. He carried her picture in his pocket. He obviously liked this Jessica kid more than he liked Amber.

"You'll have to meet her sometime," her father said. "You'd like Jessie."

"Maybe," Amber said, giving the picture back to him. She didn't want to meet the eight-year-old daughter of her father's girlfriend.

"Did you come to see Mom?" she asked suddenly.

"Yes, but I wanted to see you kids, too. Where's Justin?"

"In the basement, lifting his dumb old weights." Then she said, "Mom might lose her shop,

64

you know. She doesn't have enough money. Are you going to help her?"

"Amber." Mrs. Cantrell spoke sharply. "Let me talk to your father alone. Then you and your brother can spend time with him."

Amber went into her room and played with R.C. She tried to hear what her parents were saying, but their voices were too soft.

Justin walked past her door, sweaty from his workout.

"Are Dad and Mom still talking?" she asked. "Is he going to give her money?"

Justin shook his head. "If I know Mom, she won't take it. She wants to make it on her own."

Mr. Cantrell took them to the video arcade and gave them each two dollars to play.

Amber couldn't concentrate on any of the games. She kept thinking about that picture in her father's pocket.

Would her father put it in his wallet, along with his other pictures? Maybe he'd even take out Amber's picture and replace it with Jessica's.

SIX

The anaconda is the largest snake in the world," said David Jackson. He had a convincing fake rubber snake draped around his shoulders.

Amber stirred restlessly in her seat. Who cared about snakes?

David shook the snake's head threateningly. The girls in the front rows screamed.

"This isn't an anaconda," he explained. "It's not nearly long enough."

"Thank heavens," said Mrs. Sharp.

"But if it *was* an anaconda, it wouldn't bite you like a copperhead would. It would squee-eeze you to death."

Now David grabbed the ends of the rubber snake and wrapped them tightly around himself, as if he were being strangled by a real anaconda. He dropped to the floor, squirming and struggling.

Mrs. Sharp stood up. "Very effective, David. Does anyone else have anything for our Press Conference?"

David staggered to his feet, still battling the snake. "I could talk some more about my new garter snake, Titus—"

"Thank you, David. Your press time is up." Mrs. Sharp glanced around the classroom. "Do we have any other presentations this morning? Amber? You usually have something interesting to share with us."

Amber shook her head. She didn't have anything interesting to share. Not unless she wanted to tell the class about the picture of Jessica in her father's pocket. Or about her mother not getting any money from the bank. But she didn't want to talk about those things.

Mindy noticed Amber's silence. "What's wrong? You look kind of funny."

Amber shook her head. "Nothing." She didn't even want Mindy to know about Jessica.

Mrs. Sharp let the class get out of their seats for a few minutes to get a drink of water and sharpen pencils.

Amber stayed at her desk while the other kids milled around. She felt something heavy and rubbery on her arm. She jumped, shrieking. It was David's phony snake!

"Get that thing off me!" she squealed.

David stooped to pick up his snake. "It's not on you, Amber."

"Well, it *was*." Did David throw his stupid snake on her because he liked her? Sometimes he did weird things to show he thought she was cool. Maybe he wanted to be her boyfriend again.

Mrs. Sharp heard them. "Amber, David. What seems to be the problem? You are supposed to be at either the water fountain or the pencil sharpener, not horsing around."

"David threw his snake on my arm," Amber said.

"I did not. I dropped it accidentally. I didn't even *see* Amber sitting there."

"All right," the teacher said. "David, return to your seat."

Amber felt gloomy again. David didn't throw his snake on her to show he liked her. He didn't even know she was alive! All he cared about were snakes.

The class broke into reading teams.

Henry Hoffstedder brought his reptile book over and sat sullenly down at Mindy's desk. Mindy had left to be Lisa's reading partner.

"What page are you on?" Amber asked Henry.

"None of your beeswax."

Amber raised her hand. Every week Henry gave her a hard time. "Mrs. Sharp, Henry won't tell me what page he's on."

"Henry," said the teacher. "Cooperate with Amber. You are a team, remember? She can't help you and you can't help her if you don't work together."

Amber knew she didn't need Henry's help in reading.

So did Henry. He stuck his tongue out at her. When Amber threatened to raise her hand again, he began to read haltingly about lizards.

Even though Henry stumbled over the words, Amber concentrated on listening today. Lizards were actually kind of neat.

When Henry had finished reading two pages aloud, Amber asked him questions. Instead of making smart remarks, Henry answered the questions. No doubt about it, his reading was improving.

Then it was Amber's turn to read aloud to Henry. He seemed really interested in the story. Henry's questions made Amber think about what she had just read. *Her* reading was getting better, too.

"Henry got all the questions right," Amber reported proudly to Mrs. Sharp.

"So did Amber," Henry said.

"Good!" Mrs. Sharp praised. "Now this is a

team that works together."

After reading teams, it was time for cursive. Amber worked silently at her desk, wondering if that red-haired Jessica was up to *K* in handwriting. Did Jessica's third grade class in Philadelphia do the same things Amber's class did?

When it was time for gym, Mindy closed her cursive workbook with a sigh. "I wish we could play soccer," she said as they lined up to go to the gym. "Or even volleyball. I'm tired of gymnastics."

"I hope we do handsprings again today," Amber said. "I think I can do it right now."

But Mrs. Holland had spread the tumbling mats around the balance beam.

"We're going to walk on the beam," she told the class. "It's harder than it seems. The beam is four inches wide. That sounds plenty wide, but it is actually very narrow when you are trying to walk on it. Keeping your balance is the trick."

Mindy nudged Amber. "I'll fall off. You watch."

"No, you won't," Amber said. "It'll be just like walking on that board we put across the creek."

Mrs. Holland patted one end of the beam. "Delight, will you hop up here and show the class the proper way to walk across the beam?"

"She always picks Delight," Amber whispered to Mindy. "It's not fair."

"But Delight already knows how," Mindy argued.

Amber knew that as well as anyone, but she still thought other kids should be picked to demonstrate. Well, at least *one* other kid, with the initials A.G.C.

After Delight walked across the beam with perfect balance, the students lined up. Amber walked from one end to the other without wobbling. The beam was a cinch. What she wanted to do was work on her handspring.

While Mrs. Holland was busy helping kids jump up on the balance beam, Amber went off to one side. She didn't need a mat or anyone to spot her. She knew she wouldn't fall this time.

Amber backed up a few steps, then sprinted forward. Placing both hands on the floor, she kicked upward. But her elbows buckled and her legs came crashing down. She landed on her back with a bone-jarring thud. Her head bonked like a coconut on the hardwood floor.

Amber lay stretched out like David's rubber snake, unable to breathe or move.

Henry Hoffstedder heard Amber's head crack. "Mrs. Holland, Amber fell," he called. "I think she's hurt."

Mrs. Holland raced over to Amber.

"Are you all right?" She helped Amber to a

sitting position. "Does your head hurt?"

"Yeah. It hit the floor." Amber winced as Mrs. Holland gingerly felt the back of her head.

"I think you ought to go to the nurse. You might be getting a bump back there." She pulled Amber to her feet. "You see what happens when you work without a spotter? Class, let this be a lesson to all of you. Never attempt any tumbling routine without supervision. You can hurt yourself. Amber, you should know better."

"I was just doing a handspring," Amber explained weakly. Her head really hurt now.

"Who wants to take Amber to the clinic?" Mrs. Holland asked.

Instantly every hand was raised. Mrs. Holland chose Delight, then wrote a note for Amber to give to the school nurse.

As they walked down the hall, Delight said, "I bet you have a terrible headache. If it'd been me, I would have cried."

"It doesn't hurt that much," Amber lied, blinking back tears. It was bad enough she flubbed her handspring. She didn't want to cry in front of Delight, too.

"I fall all the time in gymnastics," Delight said. "Especially on the parallel bars."

Amber knew Delight was trying to make her feel better. She didn't say anything. It hurt to talk.

They reached the clinic.

"Hope you feel better." Delight turned and went back down the hall to their class.

Amber went inside the clinic. The nurse, Mrs. Sanders, took the note and read it. Then she examined the back of Amber's head.

"No lumps yet," she reported. "Why don't you lie down? Maybe you'll feel like returning to your class after awhile. If your headache gets worse, we'll have to call your mother. We don't want you to have a concussion."

"What's that?" Amber asked.

"A very bad headache."

"I'll be okay," Amber reassured the nurse. "You won't have to call my mother." She didn't want her mother to have to leave work on her account again.

"We'll see."

Mrs. Sanders helped Amber lie down on the cot. Paper covered the bed like a sheet. The paper crinkled whenever Amber moved her feet.

"Just yell if you need anything," the nurse said as she left.

Amber stared at the ceiling. She wasn't the least bit sleepy. She tried to figure out why she flubbed that handstand. In her mind, her legs kicked up and over perfectly.

Then she wondered if that red-haired Jessica could do gymnastics. Jessica probably did handsprings all over Philadelphia. And Amber's father probably clapped for her.

Amber turned over, tucking one hand under her aching head. She felt terrible all of a sudden. Not just her head, but all over. A tear leaked out, dribbling on the paper-covered pillow.

"Amber Gillian Cantrell!" called a cheerful voice. "What on earth are you doing in here?"

She looked up to see Ms. Lovejoy, her old teacher. She and Mindy had had Ms. Lovejoy for both first and second grade. Ms. Lovejoy was Amber's favorite teacher.

Ms. Lovejoy had understood when Amber decided to quit third grade a few months ago. Her old teacher had welcomed Amber back to her second-grade class. But Amber had found out that going back to second grade was not the answer to her problems.

"I fell in gym," she said now. "I hit my head."

Ms. Lovejoy leaned over to stroke Amber's long hair. She was wearing a soft pink sweater and smelled like roses.

"Oh, I bet that smarts," she said. "But you're strong. You'll feel better soon. I have a few minutes before I have to go back to my class. Tell me how life has been treating you."

Amber reached out to touch Ms. Lovejoy's fuzzy pink sleeve. She told her old teacher everything: that her mother might have to close the quilt shop, that her father went to see this other little girl on weekends, and that she wanted to take gymnastics lessons.

She was practically crying. She wasn't one of the most popular kids in third grade anymore. Her on-again, off-again boyfriend liked snakes better than he liked her. Her mother was worried about the quilt shop. Her brother bossed her around. And her father saw that red-haired girl more than he saw Amber.

Amber wondered where she belonged these days.

"Oh, my," Ms. Lovejoy said when Amber finished. "And now you've hurt your head on top of everything else. But try to look on the bright side."

"I can't," Amber replied, feeling thoroughly sorry for herself.

"Sure, you can! You're Amber Gillian Cantrell! There is no other third-grader in the world like you. Remember that! Things will work out. You'll see." With a final pat, Ms. Lovejoy went back to her class.

Ms. Lovejoy was right, Amber thought. There *wasn't* anybody in the world like her!

Gradually, her head stopped hurting. When Mrs. Sanders checked on her a little later, Amber was sitting up reading a magazine.

"You look chipper," the nurse pronounced. "Ready to go back to your class?"

"Yes," Amber said firmly. She was tired of feeling sorry for herself.

As she marched down the hall toward Room Six, Amber made a decision. She *would* get her place back.

In the dimness of the classroom, Amber pretended to watch the science video. She stared at the TV screen, but she wasn't really watching. Instead she thought about her problems.

How could she be important to David and her mother and her father? How could she be popular in her class again?

There was only one answer.

She would have to become famous.

As the video flickered to an end, she nudged Mindy across the aisle. "How can I become famous?"

Mindy stared at her. "I think that bump on your head is worse."

"No, really. I need to become famous. How can I do that?"

"Be a rock star," Mindy said. "They're all famous."

Amber frowned. "Not that famous. Just... regular famous."

"Regular famous? You mean like a football player?" Mindy's father was a Redskins fan. Mindy rooted for the team whenever there was a game.

"Yeah, kind of like that. Only I can't play football. What sport could I be famous at?"

She and Mindy both thought of it at the same time.

"Gymnastics," they chorused.

Mrs. Sharp, who was rewinding the video, gave them a look.

Amber lowered her voice. "I could be a famous gymnastics star. But I need lessons. How can I be a famous gymnast if I can't afford lessons?"

"Amber, this whole thing is crazy. It takes years to be famous at anything."

But Amber would not give up the idea of becoming a famous gymnast.

If she were famous, she could make commercials and give her mother the money. Then her mother wouldn't have to get a loan from the bank.

If she were famous, her father would forget about that red-haired Jessica in Philadelphia. And David Jackson would forget about snakes. The kids in Room Six would beg to sit by her at lunch.

But first she needed lessons to be a *good* gymnast, never mind being a *famous* gymnast.

She opened her mouth to ask Mindy a question, but another look from Mrs. Sharp made her close it with a snap. She would talk to Mindy later.

She didn't get another chance until they were

on the bus, on their way home. Delight, Amber, and Mindy rode the same bus. But today Delight had a special program at Tumbling Kids. Her mother picked her up at school. Delight waved good-bye as Amber and Mindy boarded the bus.

"Delight is so lucky," Amber said as they found a seat in the back. "She gets everything. She doesn't even want gymnastics lessons!"

"If you like gymnastics so much, why don't you start a gymnastics school for R.C. and Pearl?" Mindy joked.

Amber giggled. "Can you see a stuffed raccoon doing a forward roll?"

"How about a stuffed penguin walking on the balance beam?"

The picture made both girls laugh.

"We could have the school in your basement," Mindy said, still laughing. "Make a little balance beam—"

Suddenly Amber slapped her knee. "Mindy! That's it!"

"What? We're going to teach gymnastics to a bunch of stuffed animals?"

"No! We're going to teach gymnastics to a bunch of kids! There must be a lot of kids who want to take lessons! We could use our basement and charge money! Then I can give the money to Mom for her shop!"

"Amber, how is this going to help you become a famous gymnast? *You* need the lessons, remember?"

Amber bounced in her seat with excitement. "It's like being a reading tutor! Mrs. Sharp said my reading would get better because I'm helping Henry."

"I don't get it."

"If I'm a gymnastics teacher," Amber said, "I'll have to get better at gymnastics! I've been teaching Henry and my reading *is* getting better. It ought to work for gymnastics, too."

"I still don't see how," Mindy said doubtfully.

Deep inside, Amber felt the same doubts. She wondered how she could teach gymnastics when she wasn't that good herself. But it was the only plan that came to mind.

"It'll work, Mindy," she said with more confidence than she felt.

Then she remembered what Ms. Lovejoy had told her. She was Amber Gillian Cantrell, and there was no other third-grader in the world like her!

Her plan *would* work.

Chapter
SEVEN

On a small square of paper, Amber wrote *Meet me at my house.* She folded the paper into a smaller square and dropped it on Mindy's desk.

Mindy was only one desk away. Amber could have leaned over and asked her to meet her after school. But passing notes was more fun.

Mindy unfolded the square, read it, then scribbled her reply at the bottom. She passed the note back to Amber.

I'll be there, her answer said.

And she was, exactly five minutes after the bus had let them out on Carriage Street.

It was Tuesday, the day after Amber had thought of her brilliant idea. Delight had gone to her gymnastics lesson.

Amber thought, Soon I'll be taking lessons, too.

In a way, Amber was glad Delight wasn't there. She hadn't told her second-best friend about her idea. For some reason, she didn't want to tell Delight. Maybe Delight would think having a home gymnastics school was stupid.

The girls went into the Cantrells' kitchen to fix a snack.

"Don't mess up," Justin warned, as he unloaded the dishwasher. "I just cleaned in here."

"Justin is so grumpy these days," Amber whispered to Mindy. "Mom has to work late and Justin has all these chores."

"You have chores, too," Justin said, overhearing. "When are you going to get to them?"

"In a little bit," Amber said. "Mindy and I want to do something first."

"Work first, play later." Her brother gave them each one chocolate chip cookie and poured them a glass of milk. "Don't spill it." He marched into the laundry room to start the dryer, then galloped down the basement steps, closing the door behind him.

Amber looked at her lone cookie. "Justin is worse than Mom. I wish she'd find a partner so she can come home in the afternoons. When my school makes a lot of money, Mom will be able to come home again. Then I won't have to be bossed around by my brother."

"Tell Justin your school is work, not play," Mindy suggested.

"I don't want to tell him about my school at all. I want it to be a secret." She wanted to surprise her mother with the money she had earned all by herself.

Mindy drank the last of her milk. "Won't he know something is up when all these kids come to your house?"

Of course Mindy was right. It would be impossible to keep her gymnastics school a secret from her eagle-eyed brother. Especially since she needed to take over the basement. It was the only room big enough to hold her school. It was also Justin's private place.

The basement used to be Mr. Cantrell's workroom. He built a workbench and hung his tools on the walls. Mr. Cantrell took a few tools with him to his apartment in Maryland, but left the workbench.

Now Justin kept his body-building equipment in the basement. His gym consisted of a pair of dumbbells and a homemade barbell which was really a broom handle with two plastic bottles filled with sand tied to each end.

Whenever Justin got fed up with the "women" in the family, as he called them, he escaped to the basement to work out.

Amber couldn't understand why her brother

wanted to lift a broom handle with sand-filled bleach bottles over his head. It seemed pretty dumb to her.

"Your brother needs privacy," her mother explained to her once. "He's at the age where he needs some space. It's part of growing up."

So the basement became Justin's private domain. When he went downstairs and shut the door, Amber knew better than to bother him.

And now Amber needed to take over her brother's private space. She would rather walk into a lion's cage.

"Come with me," she said to Mindy.

As soon as she opened the basement door, a voice bellowed, "No girls allowed!"

"I have to ask you something," Amber said, walking slowly down the stairs. Mindy was close behind her.

"Whatever it is, it can wait."

"No it can't." She reached the bottom of the steps.

Justin was lying on his back on their father's workbench. He lifted the broom-handle barbell over his chest, then put it down to glare at Amber.

"This better be good. You know you're not supposed to be down here."

Amber cleared her throat. She had thought of a way to get her brother to give up his private place.

"I want to make a deal with you," she said

quickly, before she lost her nerve. "I need to borrow the basement for a school I'm starting. I'll pay you five cents for each student I have."

Justin sat up. "You want to *what*? Start a school in *my* basement? Are you nuts?"

"I'm not nuts. It's for Mom. If I make enough money with my school, she won't have to close the store. And I can earn money for gymnastics lessons."

"It's a gymnastics school," Mindy put in.

"A gymnastics school?" Justin echoed. "Let me get this straight: You want to take gymnastics lessons, so you're going to teach it? Now I've heard everything."

"Amber is really good," Mindy said. "She'll be a great teacher."

"And Mindy is my assistant," Amber added.

"I am?" Mindy stared at her. "I can't even do a forward roll, Amber. How am I ever going to teach that stuff?"

"I'll pay you five cents for every student, too." She would worry about Mindy later. Right now she needed a place to hold her school.

"Is it a deal?" she asked Justin hopefully. "Can I borrow the basement one hour every afternoon?"

He jiggled one end of the barbell up and down. "Why should I do this?" he demanded. "Not counting the money."

"Because we both want to help Mom," Amber said simply.

Justin sighed. "All right. I'll leave when you have your harebrained school. But how are you going to turn this place into a gym? You have to have equipment, Amber. Mats, a vault, all that stuff gymnasts use. Have you thought of that?"

"Yes, I have."

And Amber showed them how they could turn an ordinary basement into a gymnastics school.

An old leather hassock on a packing crate became the pommel horse. A board laid over two sawhorses made a passable balance beam. They didn't have blue tumbling mats, but Amber dug out the roll of foam sheeting her father used to lie on to change the oil in their car. The foam was almost as good as a regular mat.

"Mats, balance beam, vault—" Amber scanned the room. "What else do we need?"

Mindy was reading the gymnastics book Amber brought home from the library. "Rings, some kind of bars—"

"Parallel bars," Justin supplied. "We'll never make those."

"Maybe we can buy those later," Amber said. "After we've made enough money to save Mom's shop. We've got everything for now."

"Except having your head examined," Justin said dryly.

Amber was busy thinking about the posters she

and Mindy would have to make. "We have to advertise, of course."

"You forgot one other little item," Justin said.

"What?"

"Insurance."

"Insurance? What's that? What's it look like?" She had never heard of that piece of equipment before.

Justin explained. "Insurance isn't something you can see. You need it in case some kid falls and hurts himself. Then you can pay his doctor bill."

Amber still didn't understand what he was talking about. Insurance must be some sort of a doctor's bag filled with pills and bandages. They wouldn't need that.

She decided to forget about insurance. Justin was a worrywart.

"Nobody will fall," she assured him. "Mindy and I will be very good teachers. Won't we, Mindy?"

"Do I have a choice?" Mindy asked.

"No," said Amber.

With a magic marker in each hand, Amber stepped back to admire the poster she had just finished lettering.

"Perfect," she declared. "Aren't these great, Mindy?"

Mindy brushed silver glitter off her fingers.

"They do look nice. People should see them."

Eye-catching, that was what their posters were. Yesterday, Amber bought ten sheets of neon colored poster paper with her allowance—bright orange, pink, and lime green.

With the markers, she outlined "Gymnastics School. Learn to do tricks!" She and Mindy spread glue in the outlines, then filled them in with silver glitter.

"I wish we were teaching some other kind of school," Mindy grumbled. " 'Gymnastics' has too many letters in it."

"We did use a whole can of glitter," Amber agreed. "But you can see the words from far away."

Underneath the silver lettering, Amber wrote her name and address and the date of the first class, Wednesday. That was tomorrow.

"Suppose nobody comes?" Mindy said.

"They'll come," Amber said confidently. "Who doesn't want to learn tricks?"

Justin walked through the living room. He threw his hands up to his eyes when he saw the posters.

"Ow! I'm blinded!"

Amber knew he was kidding, but she wasn't sure why. "What's the matter with you?"

He put his hands down. "Nothing. But you should issue sunglasses with those posters. They knock your eyes out!"

"I want people to be able to see them," Amber said.

"Believe me, they can't miss them!" Justin noticed the date at the bottom of a green poster. "You're starting your school tomorrow?"

"Yeah. We're ready, aren't we, Mindy?"

"I know *you're* ready," Justin said. "But you ought to leave the posters up a week at least. People don't make up their minds about things right away. And little kids need to ask their parents. Also, how much are you going to charge?"

She looked at Mindy. "We never thought of that. We were too busy making posters. What sounds good? How about four, no, five dollars?"

"Five dollars?" Justin repeated. "For what? How many lessons for five dollars?"

This was getting very complicated. "Umm . . ." Amber thought. "What about five lessons for five dollars?"

"A dollar a lesson sounds awfully cheap. You have to figure in overhead, Mindy's salary. And *my* cut." Her brother grinned smugly.

Amber felt a rush of anger. "Justin, you're just trying to ruin my school! I don't even know what overhead is! All I'm going to do is teach kids gymnastics. And five lessons for five dollars is what I'm charging!"

Justin spread his hands in defeat. "Okay, okay.

Do it your way. But don't come running to me when you're in trouble."

"We aren't going to get in trouble," Amber said to Mindy when her brother had left. "Let's put up these posters before it's too dark."

A weak wintry sun was setting over the rooftops. The wind was cold.

Amber and Mindy worked fast so they could hurry back to Mindy's house for cocoa. They taped posters to all the stop signs in their neighborhood. That way nobody could miss them.

They taped the last poster on a stop sign on the other side of the creek, in Mockingbird Ridge. A girl in a bright red jacket and stocking cap was out walking.

It was Delight Wakefield.

"Hi," she greeted. "I just got back from gymnastics. What are you doing?"

Amber said nothing. When she saw Delight, she suddenly realized why she hadn't told Delight about her school.

"We're putting up posters," Mindy replied.

Delight looked at the orange poster. "A gymnastics school! Is that what you two have been up to? What a neat idea! Can I be in it?"

Amber didn't want Delight in her school. Delight would wreck the whole thing. She was so good, she would make Amber look bad.

Mindy's face brightened. "Sure you can be in it! You'd be the best teacher. Wouldn't she, Amber? Delight's the best! We'll probably have a million kids sign up."

Amber still didn't answer. She couldn't have Delight show her up. There was no way Delight would be a teacher in *her* school!

"I'm sorry," she said at last. "You can't be in our school, Delight."

"Why not?"

"Because . . . because I can't afford to pay you," Amber replied in desperation. "I'm paying Mindy, but I can't afford to pay anybody else. And somebody as good as you—you'd probably charge a lot of money—"

"I'll do it for free. It sounds like fun. I don't need the money."

"I don't either," Mindy added hastily. "It was Amber's idea to pay me because she's paying Justin rent. For the basement, I mean."

"Well," Delight said to Amber. "You won't have to worry about paying me."

"You still can't be in my school." Amber felt more trapped by the second. "I can only have two teachers. It has to do with overhead. My brother said."

Delight's eyebrows drew together. "I don't believe you, Amber Cantrell. You don't *want* me in your school. Why don't you just say so?"

"I—"

"I know why you don't want me in your school," Delight said. "You're jealous because I take gymnastics."

"That's not it," Amber said lamely.

She *was* jealous, but she didn't want to admit it. After all, Delight was her second-best friend. But Amber was tired of watching Delight always be picked in gym class to demonstrate routines. In Amber's school, *Amber* would be the star.

Delight rushed on, her face pink with anger. "You've been acting funny lately and now I know why. Tell the truth, Amber. You don't want to be friends with me, do you?"

Amber knew Delight's feelings were hurt. She felt terrible, but she simply stood there, watching her breath blow out in frosty puffs.

"Amber!" Mindy prompted. "*Say* something!"

"She doesn't have to say anything," Delight said huffily. "She doesn't want to be friends anymore and neither do I. From now on, Amber Gillian Cantrell, you and I are enemies!"

EIGHT

At school the next day a crowd of kids gathered around Amber's desk. They had all seen Amber's silver-glitter posters around the neighborhood.

"A gymnastics school!" exclaimed Carly. "What a neat idea!"

"Mindy helped me think of it," Amber said modestly. "She's a teacher in the school, too."

"But it's really Amber's school," Mindy put in. "It's at her house."

Amber felt great. All the kids were hanging around *her* desk. She was popular again!

"I wish I could take lessons," said Lisa. "I love gymnastics."

"Why don't you?" Amber dug out her

clipboard. It was really Justin's clipboard. She had borrowed it so she could write down the names of the students who enrolled in her school.

"Are you going to be in my school?" she asked Lisa.

Lisa shook her head sadly. "I don't think my mother will let me. She says we have to save money for Christmas."

"Our prices are very reasonable," Amber said. She had learned that line from a TV commercial.

Henry Hoffstedder perched on the edge of Amber's desk. "How much are you charging?"

"Five dollars for five lessons," Mindy replied.

"What a gyp! With Amber as a teacher, you ought to teach for free!"

Amber pushed Henry off her desk. "If you don't mind. I'm trying to run a business here." She looked around at the group. "Is anyone going to sign up for my school?"

David Jackson raised his hand.

"David." Amber began printing his name on her clipboard. "D-A-V—"

"Well, not me exactly," he said. "My snake Titus."

Mindy screamed. The other girls shrieked at the mention of David's pet garter snake.

Amber glared at him. "No snakes allowed."

"Aw, come on, Amber," Henry said, sputtering

with laughter. "Don't you want Titus for a student? You should give him a discount!"

In her most businesslike tone, Amber said, "Does anyone else want to sign up for gymnastics lessons? Any *humans,* I mean."

David grinned at her just like he used to.

Amber found herself grinning back. She couldn't stay annoyed at David. He was just teasing her. Maybe he liked her again.

"Hey," he said suddenly. "The Cobras are meeting during lunch. You want to come?"

Her heart leaped. David was practically asking her to join his snake club! He really *did* like her.

"I'm not sure," she said. "Maybe."

She wasn't really interested in snakes, but just being asked made her feel great.

Then she noticed Delight across the room. Delight was stowing her knapsack under her desk. She did not look over at the crowd of kids around Amber's desk. When she had finished putting her things away, she stared straight ahead at the blackboard.

Carly went over to her own desk. "Delight, what do you think about Amber's gymnastics school?"

"Not much," Delight replied.

David said, "Hey! I thought you guys were friends."

"Amber is not *my* friend," Delight told him.

"We are enemies."

"Fight! Fight! Amber and Delight!" hooted Henry Hoffstedder.

Amber's neck burned. Now everybody knew she and Delight weren't friends anymore.

If only Delight were *awful* at gymnastics, like Mindy. Then Amber would let her be a teacher, too. But if she let Delight in her school, Delight would be the star. It wouldn't be Amber's school anymore.

"Why don't you start your own school?" Lisa asked Delight.

Amber wanted to tell Lisa to mind her own beeswax. If Delight started a gymnastics school, Amber's school didn't stand a chance.

"I have better things to do," Delight replied icily.

When Delight glanced over at her, Amber turned to face the blackboard. She could act snooty, too.

Just then Mrs. Sharp came into the room with a batch of new worksheets.

"All right, class," she said. "Let's get settled. Henry, in your seat, please, not on top of it. Amber, put away that clipboard. It does not look like schoolwork."

The class did math and then worked on their second canned book report. When it was time for recess, Amber marched down to the gym, hoping she looked like a gymnastics teacher.

Today Mrs. Holland showed them how to vault. Delight demonstrated. She ran very fast toward the pommel horse, sprang up with her hands on the horse, then swung both legs over. The rest of the class took turns vaulting.

Leaping over the leather pommel horse was hard, yet Amber aced it. But she still couldn't do a handspring. Neither could Mindy.

Amber asked the teacher to help them do a handspring.

"Not right now, Amber," Mrs. Holland said. "I have to spot the kids vaulting."

Amber knew the teacher had to stand beside the pommel horse, in case a student fell. She also knew she and Mindy weren't allowed to do any stunts without the teacher to spot *them*, in case they fell.

"Forget it," Mindy said, rubbing her knee. She had banged into the pommel horse instead of flying over the way Amber did. "We just won't teach handsprings."

"I can show you how to do a handspring," said a voice.

Amber and Mindy turned around.

Delight was doing warm-up exercises on the mat next to them.

"You'll get in trouble," Amber told her. "Nobody's allowed to do anything without the teacher."

"I wasn't talking to you," Delight said, looking pointedly at Mindy. "Mindy, I'll show *you* what you're doing wrong."

She glanced over at Mrs. Holland. Satisfied the teacher was busy, Delight performed a perfect handspring.

"See?" said Delight, still ignoring Amber. "It's really easy."

"For you, maybe," Mindy said skeptically. "I can't even do a forward roll!"

Amber was tempted to tell on Delight. Delight was always the one chosen to do demonstrations. If Amber told Mrs. Holland what Delight did, maybe the teacher would pick Amber to give demonstrations.

But Amber hated tattletales. Instead she said to Delight, "I don't care if you do handsprings all the way home. You still can't be in my school!"

"I don't want to be in your stale old school," Delight said haughtily. "Not even if you begged me!"

"Fat chance!"

"We'll see!"

"Stop it!" Mindy cried. "This is so stupid! Let's all be friends again."

"It's too late," Amber said. "Delight and I are enemies. Forever and ever!"

Mrs. Holland called Delight to demonstrate vaulting again. Delight ran over.

"She doesn't know everything," Amber said, watching Delight sail over the pommel horse. "You wait. Every kid in the neighborhood will come to my school. That'll show Miss Perfect."

Three kids.

Only three students showed up for the first day of Amber's gymnastics school: Mindy's little sister Karen, Karen's best friend, Elise, and Elise's older brother, Ricky. Karen and Elise were both four. Ricky was six.

Amber took her students down to the basement, printed their names on her clipboard, then asked them each to pay for their lessons. Justin had advised her to get the money up front.

"Five dollars for five lessons. Karen, where's your money?"

Karen twisted the hair of the doll she had brought. "I don't have to pay. My sister is the teacher."

Mindy shrugged. "She is my sister, Amber. How can we charge my own sister?"

Amber couldn't argue with that logic. "All right, Karen. Elise, what about your money?"

Elise dug into the pocket of her jeans. She pulled out a gummy quarter and offered it to Amber.

"A quarter? Is that all you have?" Sighing, Amber put the quarter in the Band-Aid tin she was using as a bank. She had pictured the Band-Aid tin stuffed full of five-dollar bills.

She dropped the quarter into her bank. It gave a lonely-sounding plunk at the bottom.

"Okay, uh—" Amber had forgotten the boy's name.

"Ricky!" the boy shouted, as if Amber were deaf as well as forgetful. "Nobody said anything about paying money! I thought we were just going to have fun here."

"Of course you have to pay," Amber said. "It's a school and you have to pay for the lessons."

Ricky pointed to Elise and Karen. "They said it was a play group. I came along because I have to stay with my sister."

Amber was confused. "Didn't you read the posters? This is a gymnastics school."

"I didn't see any posters."

Amber turned to Mindy. "What did you tell these kids?"

"I said we were having a fun time at the house across the street," Mindy replied. "It was the only way to get them to come. Don't complain. You wouldn't have any students at all if it wasn't for me!"

"But none of them is paying!" Amber exclaimed. "I'm not running a free school!"

"I'll pay," Ricky said. "But only if I like this school. It better be more fun than real school."

"All right." Amber sighed. Obviously no one

else was coming. She might as well accept these three as her first students.

Mindy rounded up the students to show them around the "gymnasium."

Amber woefully shook the Band-Aid bank. Twenty-five cents. That's all she had. She owed fifteen cents to Justin for letting her use the basement. And another fifteen cents to Mindy.

She wasn't very good in math, but she could add. Fifteen cents plus fifteen cents equaled thirty cents. And she only had twenty-five cents. She'd been in business less than an hour, and she was already five cents in the hole.

How would she ever earn enough money to help her mother keep the quilt shop? How would she earn enough to pay for classes at Tumbling Kids?

Maybe I'll get more kids tomorrow, she thought hopefully.

"All right, class." She clapped her hands to get their attention.

Karen and Elise were playing with their dolls on the tumbling mat. Ricky was climbing on the balance beam.

"Get down from there!" Amber yelled at him. "Never, ever, *ever* use the equipment without supervision. That's Rule Number One."

"That's a stupid rule," Ricky said. "What's Rule Number Two?"

"Rule Number Two is don't get smart with your teacher. Now *get down*."

"That rule is even dumber." Ricky reluctantly jumped off the balance beam. He ran over and swiped Elise's doll.

"Give that back!" Elise cried. "Amber, make him give me back my doll!"

Amber knew why grown-ups complained of headaches. "Ricky, give Elise back her doll. Karen and Elise, put those dolls away. We're not here to play."

"I thought we were going to do fun stuff," Ricky said.

"We are. But you have to listen to me." She pointed to Mindy. "My assistant will demonstrate a forward roll."

"I can't *do* a forward roll," Mindy cried. "You know that!"

"Mrs. Holland always asks Delight to demonstrate," Amber said testily. "That's what assistants do."

"Not this assistant," Mindy said, getting testy herself.

Karen and Elise were playing with their dolls again. Ricky had vanished.

"Where's Ricky?" Amber cried, panicked. "Ricky! Where are you? Come out right now!"

Ricky appeared from behind the furnace.

Cobwebs laced his blond hair. He grinned at Amber.

"Did I scare you, teacher?"

Amber felt like running away. The school was not working out like she thought it would. Her assistant was sulky, two of the students refused to pay, and none of them would listen to her.

"Okay!" she barked. "Now we're going to learn to do a forward roll. All of you, watch me. Then I'll let you try."

She squatted at the edge of the mat and rolled. Something sharp dug in her back. When she looked back, she saw she had rolled on Karen's doll.

"You squashed her!" Karen accused.

"I did not. If anything, she jabbed me." Amber made the students line up at the edge of the mat. "Karen, you go first."

"I want to go first," said Ricky. "Girls always get to go first."

"That's because they don't make as much noise as boys. All right, Ricky. You can go first. Mindy is your spotter. She will stay by you and make sure you don't fall."

"How can I fall? I'm rolling on the floor." Ricky squatted on his heels, leaned forward on his palms, and rolled.

Amber was surprised that Ricky did it right on his first try. Karen and Elise did perfect forward rolls, too.

"Have you guys had lessons?" Amber wanted to know.

"Why would we be here?" Ricky said. He was very smart for his age, Amber decided. Maybe a little too smart.

Next they did backward rolls. Again, the students performed them perfectly.

"What are we going to do now?" asked Elise.

Amber had already used up the lessons for the first two days of school. If her students kept learning this fast, they would know all she knew by the end of the week. What else could she teach them?

"School's over," she announced, herding them all toward the stairs. "See you tomorrow."

"My mother said you had to keep me a whole hour," Ricky grumbled.

"I'm not your baby sitter," Amber said tartly.

If she were Ricky's baby sitter, at least she would get *paid*.

Chapter NINE

Crash!

The keg of nails hit the cement floor with a sound like a hardware store falling down.

Amber jumped. "Ricky!" she cried. "*Now* what have you done?"

"Sorry." He gave her an angelic grin. "It just slipped when I tried to stand on it."

"You weren't supposed to be standing on anything," Amber scolded. "You were *supposed* to be doing forward rolls, like Karen and Elise."

He shrugged. "I got bored."

It was the second day of Amber's gymnastics school. When her students had arrived, Amber looked eagerly to see if any others had joined the group. No one had. She still had only three students—Karen, Elise, and Ricky.

Yesterday evening, Justin had collected his fifteen cents in basement "rent."

"This is *all*?" he'd complained. "All you have are three lousy kids?"

"That was today. Maybe more will come tomorrow."

He'd jingled the three nickels in his palm. "This is hardly worth letting you have my basement. Those kids better not wreck the place."

"They won't," Amber had promised, hiding her crossed fingers behind her back.

She had paid Mindy, too. At first Mindy refused to take the money, but Amber insisted. "A business deal is a business deal," she'd told her friend.

Amber hoped more students would enroll in her school. How else would she save her mother's shop and earn money for lessons at Tumbling Kids?

Maybe tomorrow I'll get more students, Amber thought as she led the three children down to the basement. A few kids *her* age would be nice.

The little girls were okay. When they weren't practicing forward and backward rolls on the foam mat, they were teaching their dolls how to tumble.

But that Ricky!

Amber didn't see how his mother could put up with him. No wonder his mother sent him with Elise—she was probably glad to get rid of him for an hour. Still, Amber's school was *not* a play group. She wondered if she should send a note home with Ricky and Elise. Maybe their mother didn't know her kids were taking gymnastics.

"Ricky, when are you and your sister going to pay me?" Amber asked him.

"I still don't know if I like this school yet," he replied breezily.

"Your sister likes it," Amber said.

"Girls like anything," he stated.

That was before Ricky turned over the keg of nails. Before that, he hammered a tune on an upturned bucket. And before *that*, he found Mr. Cantrell's saw and was about to hack a hole in the stairs when Mindy caught him.

Now Amber and Mindy exchanged a weary glance. Nails were everywhere. Someone would have to pick them up.

"Honestly, that kid," Mindy said under her breath.

Teaching gymnastics—or anything, for that matter—to three lively little kids was harder than Amber had ever imagined. She didn't have enough eyes to keep track of Ricky. When he wasn't getting in trouble, he was pestering her to teach him something harder than a forward roll.

Very quickly he and the girls mastered cartwheels, handstands, and headstands. Ricky could even walk on his hands.

"They must be born knowing this stuff," Amber said to Mindy, as they scraped nails into a snow shovel. "I don't know what else to teach them. If I show them how to vault and walk on the balance beam, that'll be it."

Mindy nodded. "Mrs. Holland didn't let us get on the balance beam or the vault for a long time."

"I know! And this is only the second day!"

With both of them guiding the handle, they pushed the nail-filled snow shovel into a corner. They didn't have time to dump the nails back into the keg. Amber hoped Justin or her mother wouldn't see the mess and ask questions.

Justin would be furious if he knew that Ricky was into all his weight-lifting stuff and their father's tools.

But Amber's mother would be even more furious if she found out about the school. Neither Justin nor Amber were permitted to have kids over while their mother was working. Mindy could come over because she was practically family. But not a bunch of little kids. And certainly not a troublemaker like Ricky.

The only good thing about her mother's long hours, Amber reasoned as she leaned the snow shovel in the corner, was that she was too busy to come down into the basement and see what was going on.

"What can we do now?" asked Elise.

"We're going to do more handstands," Amber said. She still had a half hour to teach. Why did these kids have to learn so fast?

"I don't want to do handstands," Ricky whined. "I want to walk on this." He crooked one leg over the balance beam.

Amber hurried over and dragged him off the apparatus. The board wobbled on its sawhorse supports.

"You're not ready for the balance beam yet," she told him. "You have to be really, really good at handstands and cartwheels before you can walk on the balance beam."

"I'm already good at cartwheels," he argued. "Why can't I walk on the balance beam?"

In desperation Amber snapped, "Because I'm the teacher and I say you can't! That's why!" Now she knew why grown-ups said things like that.

Karen and Elise looked at her, surprised. Ricky's lower lip quivered in a pout.

"Today we're going to review what we've learned so far," Mindy said quickly. Mrs. Sharp often gave the class reviews. They would go over material they had already covered.

Amber flashed Mindy a grateful glance. Mindy handled little kids better than she did. Probably because she had two little sisters.

While the kids were tumbling, Mindy said to

Amber, "You really ought to let Delight be a teacher. She'd have all kinds of stuff for them to learn."

"Never! Delight and I are enemies," Amber said. "And that is that."

At last Amber's school was out. The little kids and Mindy went home. Justin fixed microwave lasagna for supper. Mrs. Cantrell came home from work and they ate.

"How's it going?" Justin asked.

Amber nearly dropped her fork. For a second she thought he was speaking to her. But he had promised to keep her school a secret.

Mrs. Cantrell put her head in her hands. "Well, I'm starting a holiday sale tomorrow. That sale might continue into a close-out sale."

"Is it that bad, Mom?" Justin looked concerned.

"If I don't find an investor soon—someone to replace my business partner—I'll have to close the shop," she replied. "I'm already behind in my rent...." She looked at them and smiled. "But you don't want to hear such dreary news. Not this close to Christmas."

The doorbell rang.

"Oh, that must be your father," Mrs. Cantrell said. "He called me at the shop and said he was dropping by. I think he wants to take you kids out for ice cream. He probably won't make it this weekend again."

Amber ran to the door. Her father greeted her with a big hug. Cold air clung to his wool coat.

"Daddy! Mom is having an awful time! Did you know?"

"Yes, I do know. I offered to help her out, but—" He turned his palms upward. "Your mother is a very independent woman. She wants to work this out for herself. I admire her for that."

He put his arm around Amber's shoulder. She sniffed the smell of his after-shave. Her father always smelled so good! Even though she knew he wouldn't visit her and Justin this weekend, she was glad to see him.

"Did you bring me anything?" she asked automatically.

Then she remembered the last time she had asked that question and had found the photograph of Jessica. He probably brought little presents to *her* now.

"Of course I have something for my pumpkin." Her father took a small package from his coat pocket. "You put these on your shoelaces. Jessie says all the kids in Philly wear them. You'll be the first in your school!"

Amber stared at the bright-colored disks. They did look neat. And she loved to be the first to try a new fad. But she didn't like being second in her father's heart. Obviously that red-haired Jessica girl helped her father pick them out.

"What kind of ice cream do you want?" Mr. Cantrell asked.

"I don't care," Amber replied dully. Suddenly, she wasn't as excited about seeing her father.

"Do you want me to show you how the buttons go on your shoelaces?" He started to open the cellophane.

"No," Amber said. "I can figure it out."

She had figured out a lot of things lately. That her father liked this Jessica kid better than he liked her. That teaching a gymnastics school was hard work. And that best friends sometimes became enemies.

And she was no closer to getting a yellow leotard or real gymnastics lessons.

On Friday Amber wore the colored buttons on her shoelaces. At first she wasn't going to, but then she decided she liked them. Even if that Jessica kid had picked them out, Amber thought the buttons were cute.

On the bus, Mindy admired Amber's shoelace buttons. Carly and Lisa admired them in the classroom. Even David said he thought his snake would like the colored disks on a string to play with.

"They come all the way from Philadelphia," Amber told the kids around her desk. "My dad brought them to me. He said all the kids up there are wearing these on their shoelaces."

"How does your dad know what kids are wearing in Philadelphia?" Henry Hoffstedder asked rudely.

Amber's face turned red. The other kids knew her parents were divorced and that her father lived in Maryland. But she didn't want the others to know that her father went to Philadelphia to see another girl when he had a perfectly good daughter right here in Virginia.

"Amber's father notices things," said Delight. She was passing by on her way to the pencil sharpener. "Not like you, Henry."

"Same to you, only more of it!" Henry retorted.

Amber was surprised that Delight was standing up for her. Especially since they were enemies now.

In gym, Amber saw Delight staring at her feet. She figured Delight admired her colored shoelace buttons, too.

It was fun wearing something new that no one else had. She was glad her father gave them to her, even if another girl did pick them out.

Amber liked the way the colored disks flashed when she did a cartwheel. Then she tried to do a front handspring, but fell over in a tangle of legs. *Why* couldn't she do a handspring?

Later, at lunch, Amber caught Mindy in a whispered conversation with Delight.

"What were you two talking about?" Amber asked her.

Mindy unwrapped her peanut butter sandwich. "Nothing," she said casually.

"Delight and I are still enemies," Amber warned.

"But *I'm* not enemies with Delight," Mindy said.

Something in her tone made Amber change the subject. Mindy didn't always do everything Amber told her these days. They were still best-best friends, but Mindy was more her own person.

When school was out, Amber wanted to play with R.C. and Pearl.

"You have to teach school," Mindy reminded her.

Amber had forgotten about her gymnastics school. After two days, she was tired of teaching. Maybe no one would show up and she wouldn't have to.

But Karen, Elise, and Ricky were right on time.

"Are we going to do the balance beam today?" Ricky asked brightly.

"No, we are not," Amber replied. "Today we're going to learn a combination. That's where you do all the things you've learned, only you put them together. I'll show you."

She pulled the foam mat into the center of the room.

"I'm going to do a forward roll, with a handstand in middle, then a backward roll with a headstand in the middle."

Mrs. Holland had taught Amber's class their first combination that day. Amber hoped she could remember and do it for her own students.

She heard the distant chime of the doorbell.

"I'll get it," Mindy said quickly. She was already running upstairs.

Amber pitched into her forward roll, rising into a handstand with no problem. But she didn't have enough momentum in her backward roll to kick her legs up into a headstand. She tumbled over sideways.

Ricky laughed as if she were a clown in a circus.

Amber jumped up, frowning. "It isn't funny—" she began. Then she saw who Mindy had brought downstairs with her.

Delight.

"Look who's here!" Mindy said, a bit too cheerfully.

"You cooked this up," Amber accused. "You and Delight, at lunch today. You told her she could come to my school!"

"While I'm here, I could show your class that combination," said Delight.

She crouched at the edge of the foam mat, then performed a flawless forward roll–handstand, backward roll–headstand.

"I didn't say you could do that!" Amber shouted.

She could hardly believe Delight's nerve, taking over her class like she owned the place! "Anyway, I've decided not to teach that combination. We're going to do something else. And you have to leave!"

"Oh, Amber," Mindy said. "Let Delight stay. She's better at gymnastics than you and me."

"Only because she takes real lessons!" Amber cried. Tears stung her eyes. "You get to do everything," she yelled at Delight. "You're so lucky and you don't even know it!"

"I don't even want to take gymnastics," Delight fired back. "I'm sick of taking lessons. But my mother makes me. You know who's lucky? You are, Amber Cantrell. *You* get to do everything, not me."

"I don't get to do anything!"

"Yes, you do! You and Mindy are always doing neat stuff together. I came over today because Mindy said you needed help. And...because I missed you guys." Delight let out a shaky breath. "I wish I could be with you and Mindy all the time."

Amber looked at her enemy. She didn't feel so angry anymore.

But before she could say anything, a crash sounded behind them.

Ricky again! Amber thought, expecting another mess to clean up.

But this time, it wasn't a keg of nails that had fallen.

Chapter
TEN

Ricky lay sprawled on the cement floor.

One of the sawhorses that supported the balance beam board had toppled over. The board straddled Ricky's body like a playground teeter-totter.

He was whimpering.

Amber ran over to him. "Are you okay?" she asked, pulling the board off of him. "Can you sit up?"

"My head!" Ricky wailed.

Mindy and Delight helped him sit up. Karen explained what happened.

"He was climbing on the balance beam. Me and Elise told him he shouldn't, but he did it anyway. And then the board went up and he fell over backward."

Amber knelt beside Ricky and took his hand.

"Where does your head hurt?" she asked.

"It hurts in the back," he said, sobbing. "Don't touch it!"

Amber looked over his head at Mindy and Delight. "I don't know what to do," she said helplessly.

"We should call his mother," Delight said.

"Good idea!" Amber headed for the stairs. Ricky's mother would come and take him home.

"She's not home!" Ricky cried. "She went to the store."

"Amber," Mindy said. "Ricky ought to go to the doctor."

"Or the emergency room," added Delight.

Amber wrung her hands. "Justin told me somebody would get hurt. I didn't believe him. And now somebody is hurt!"

"You can't think about that now," Delight told her. "You have to take care of Ricky. He might have a—what is it people get when they crack their head?"

"It's called a confession or something like that," Amber said. "Remember when I fell that day in gym? The nurse thought I had one. But I didn't."

Ricky's crying grew louder. Elise offered him her doll, but he pushed it away.

Amber felt like crying herself. "My mother's at work. I guess I'll have to find Justin."

"I could run across the street and get my

mother," Mindy offered. "The baby's sick, though. She may not want to leave her."

"Wait," Delight said. "My mother is home. She'll know what to do. I'll call her."

She ran upstairs to phone her mother.

Within five minutes, Mrs. Wakefield was at the Cantrell house. She gently examined Ricky's head.

"Getting a bump there, sport," she said soothingly. "Your mother isn't home, is that right?"

Ricky nodded. He had stopped crying when Mrs. Wakefield picked him up and rocked him in her lap.

Mrs. Wakefield spoke to Amber. "Your mother doesn't know anything about this...school, does she?" Amber shook her head miserably. "Okay. We won't bother her just yet. Ricky, how about a little ride to the clinic? Afterwards, I'll buy you a frozen yogurt."

"Rocky Road," Ricky said. "That's my favorite kind."

Mrs. Wakefield organized Operation Head Check, as she called it. Mindy took Karen home. Elise went with them.

Justin came in from playing basketball and heard the whole story.

"I knew this school idea wouldn't work," he said to Amber. "I should have told Mom. Now you're in for it."

They all piled into Mrs. Wakefield's van and

drove to the clinic. Ricky sat up front with Mrs. Wakefield. Amber, Delight, and Justin climbed into the back.

In the waiting room, Amber plucked Mrs. Wakefield's sleeve. She had just had a horrible thought.

"I don't have insurance," she whispered. "Am I going to get in trouble?"

"Don't worry about it," Mrs. Wakefield assured her with a pat. "Everything will be all right."

But Amber wasn't so sure.

Especially when Mrs. Wakefield called Amber's mother at the shop.

"I'm sorry, dear," she said to Amber. "But I had to tell her. The accident happened in her house. But Ricky's fine. He just has a big goose egg."

After getting the number from information, Mrs. Wakefield called Ricky's mother and reported that her son had been in an accident but was okay.

When Ricky was released from the clinic, Mrs. Wakefield took them all to get frozen yogurt. Then they drove to Ricky's house.

Ricky's mother hugged her son, then thanked Mrs. Wakefield. She seemed confused over the situation.

"I thought he was in a play group at Karen Alexander's house," she said.

"The play group was really a gymnastics school

at Amber Cantrell's house," Mrs. Wakefield said, putting her arm around Amber. "I don't think Mrs. Cantrell knew about it either. I've written her number on Ricky's emergency room bill. I'm sure you'll want to talk to her and settle this."

Amber listened with growing dismay. Her mother would probably have to pay that emergency room bill. She had no idea a little fall would cause so much trouble.

Then they drove the two blocks to the Cantrell house. Amber's heart sank when she saw her mother's car parked in the driveway. So far Mrs. Wakefield had taken care of everything. But now Amber had to face the music.

"A gymnastics school in my basement!" Mrs. Cantrell exclaimed as soon as they entered the house. "Amber, what could you have been thinking of? And that flimsy contraption you made. Didn't you realize someone would get hurt on that thing?"

"It's a balance beam," Amber said in a small voice. "I didn't think anybody would get hurt."

"And you charged money to these children?" her mother demanded.

"Five dollars for five lessons. But nobody paid, except Elise. And she only paid a quarter."

Her mother sighed. "You will give Elise back her quarter, of course."

"I can't," Amber admitted. "I gave fifteen cents

of it to Justin to rent the basement. And I gave the rest to Mindy because she was my assistant."

Now her mother turned to Justin. "Justin, you knew about Amber's enterprise all along and didn't tell me?"

"Amber made me promise not to," Justin said defensively.

"That's no excuse, Justin. I counted on you to watch Amber. I counted on you both to be responsible."

"Don't blame me!" Justin countered. "Amber was the one who wanted to earn money for gymnastics lessons."

"Amber, is this true?" Mrs. Cantrell asked. "You started this school to earn money for gymnastics lessons?"

Amber nodded. "And a yellow leotard. But I was going to give the rest of the money to you. So you can keep the shop." She felt terrible she had caused her mother more trouble instead of helping her.

Her mother put her head in her hands. "Oh dear," she said wearily. "I guess I'm the one to blame. I thought we could all hang together while I worked extra hours at the shop. But I can see I was asking too much."

Just then Mrs. Wakefield cleared her throat. She and Delight had been standing in the doorway the whole time.

"Why don't I fix us a nice cup of tea?" she said to Amber's mother. "Let the kids go into the other room for a bit."

Amber didn't need any further encouragement. She and Delight went into the living room. Justin ducked into his bedroom.

Amber slumped in a chair. "What a mess. Now my mom will lose her shop. And I'll never get gymnastics lessons. And it's all my fault."

"Don't feel bad," Delight said, sitting on the rug.

"I do feel bad. I feel awful." She looked at Delight. Delight had been a good friend that afternoon, calling her mother when Amber didn't know what to do.

"I don't want to be enemies anymore," she said. "Can we be friends again?"

"I never really wanted to be enemies," Delight said. "It's just that you acted so mean over your school."

"I'm sorry," Amber apologized. "I guess I was jealous because you're so good in gymnastics. You're good at everything you do."

Delight shook her head. "Not everything. There's one thing you do a lot better than anyone I know, Amber Cantrell."

"What's that?"

"Think up neat ideas. Who else would have thought of starting a gymnastics school?"

Amber laughed. "It wasn't my idea at all! It was Mindy's!"

Delight laughed too. "Well, usually it's you! I wish I could come up with neat stuff like you do. You and Mindy have the most fun."

"You'll have fun with us," Amber told her. "Now that we're friends again. Come on. Let's go in my room and play Parcheesi."

They had almost finished the second game when Mrs. Wakefield called Delight.

"Time to go home," she said. "I have to fix supper." She spoke to Amber's mother, who walked them to the door. "Think about my offer. This would solve both our problems."

"I will," Mrs. Cantrell promised. "And I'll call you later. Thanks again for helping during the crisis."

When Mrs. Wakefield and Delight had left, Mrs. Cantrell closed the door and leaned against it.

"I think our prayers have been answered," she said happily. "Delight's mother wants to be my partner."

"In your shop?" Amber asked.

Her mother nodded. "She's been looking for some interesting work ever since they moved here. She loves antiques and decorating. Her house shows she has great style. Plus she is willing to invest in the shop. I won't have to sell it!"

"Mom, that's great!" Amber hugged her

mother. "Then everything is okay now?"

"Well, that depends. No more gymnastics school in our basement?"

Amber crossed her heart. "No more gymnastics school." She was tired of teaching kids like Ricky.

"And will you take more responsibility and be a team player?" her mother asked. "It's the only way this family will work."

Amber remembered how Henry Hoffstedder used to fool around during reading team time. Then he began to work with Amber and his reading improved. She didn't fight with him as much either. There must be something to this team business, Amber thought.

"I'll be a team player," she promised. "I'll even do everything Justin tells me."

Justin came out of his room. "That'll be the day. Did I hear something about Mrs. Wakefield being your partner?"

"If I accept her offer. And I believe I will." Mrs. Cantrell kissed Amber's nose, then patted Justin's shoulder. "Let's go out for pizza tonight. We deserve it."

Amber's spirits lifted. She was glad everything had turned out all right.

At the pizza parlor, Mrs. Cantrell told Amber something that made her feel even better.

"We can't afford gymnastics lessons at Tumbling Kids," said Mrs. Cantrell. "But Mrs. Wakefield told me about classes the county recreation department offers. They are very reasonable. You should be able to start gymnastics lessons in January, when the new quarter begins. That will be my Christmas present to you."

"I can? Oh, Mom!" Amber ran around the table to throw her arms around her mother. "That's the best Christmas present in the world!"

Justin grabbed Amber's arm and raised it up, like a winning prizefighter's. "The next Olympic champion!"

He wasn't such a bad brother, Amber thought. He *had* gone along with her scheme to have a gymnastics school in the basement and even helped set it up.

Amber finished her pizza, glowing with happiness. Almost all of her problems were solved.

Her heart dipped a bit when she thought of the red-haired girl in Philadelphia, the girl her father liked better than her. She might become a famous gymnast, but it would take a long time. She couldn't think of any other way to get her father's attention.

On Saturday, Amber was surprised when her mother said her father had called the night before.

"He'll be here shortly to take you and Justin

back to his apartment for the weekend," said Mrs. Cantrell.

"He's not going to Philadelphia?" Amber asked.

"Apparently not," her mother answered.

Her father picked them up on time. He and Justin chatted about the last Redskins game as they plowed through holiday traffic. Amber stared out the window at the passing scenery, quiet for once.

When they arrived at Mr. Cantrell's apartment in Maryland, Mr. Cantrell handed Amber a big white box tied with a gold ribbon.

"What's this?" she said.

"An early Christmas present. Go on, open it."

Amber untied the gold ribbon and opened the box. Inside, folded in tissue paper, was a yellow leotard.

"Oh, Dad! How did you know?" she cried. "I've been wanting a yellow leotard *forever*!"

"I wouldn't be a very good father if I didn't know what my own daughter wanted for Christmas," he said, laughing. "Your mom told me you're taking gymnastics lessons after Christmas. I figured you'd need a leotard. And I remembered that yellow is one of your favorite colors."

"Can I see your wallet?" Amber asked suddenly.

Her father reached into his back pocket for his billfold. "I don't have much money—"

"I don't want to see your money," Amber told

126

him. "I want to see your pictures."

Her father opened a flap. "I only carry two pictures," he said.

Inside the flap were two photographs: Amber's third grade picture and Justin's eighth grade picture. No picture of Jessica.

"You only have pictures of us," Amber said, surprised.

"You're my only kids," her father said, putting his wallet in his pocket again.

"Are you going to be here for Christmas?" Amber asked. What if he wanted to spend Christmas with his lady friend and Jessica?

Her father hugged her. "Right here."

Amber hugged him back. Her stuffed raccoon was nice to hug, but hugging her father was nicer because he hugged back. She rested her head against his chest, in that special place her head had always fit. She knew where she belonged, too—with her family. And though her family might not live under the same roof, she knew both her father and her mother loved her.

The day before Christmas vacation was the last day of gymnastics.

Mrs. Holland, who wore jingle bells instead of a whistle around her neck, made an announcement.

"I am very impressed with my third grade

gymnasts," she said. "You all did exceptionally well. I would like to continue working with you. So I'm starting a gymnastics squad. We will meet after school one day a week and work on the equipment."

"I want to join," Amber said immediately. "Will you guys join, too?" she asked Mindy and Delight.

"I will," said Delight.

"I'm not very good," Mindy said hesitantly.

"But you'll improve," Amber encouraged. "And we'll be a team."

Being a team player, she had discovered, was a lot better than being a star on her own. This way, she would have her friends around her.

Then, for no reason except that she was happy, Amber sprang forward onto the blue mat and performed a perfect handspring.

"I did it!" she cried triumphantly.

She heard applause. Delight and Mindy were clapping.

Amber bowed. Okay, so it wasn't hundreds of people clapping for her. Only two. Her two best friends in the world.

And for now, that was enough.